Finally Michael spoke. 'Just what the hell are you doing here?' he asked in a low voice.

Val clutched her handbag to her chest. 'I was just leaving,' she said.

He eyed her narrowly. 'I'm surprised you had the nerve to come here,' he said in a flat, toneless voice.

Val raised her chin. 'I told you,' she said defiantly. 'Your mother invited me. It *is* her house.'

When he made no reply and merely continued to stare at her as though she were some species of loathsome insect, Val suddenly saw red. 'If you have something to say to me, Michael, then you'd better come right out with it.'

He raised one heavy black eyebrow. 'You may have fooled my mother into believing that innocent act of yours, but you'll find that I'm not quite so gullible.'

Books you will enjoy
by ROSEMARY HAMMOND

MY DESTINY

When detective Stephen Ryan made it clear that he wanted to see more of her, Joanna couldn't help but remember the last man she'd loved. Three years ago she had been married to Ross, also a policeman, and he'd died in the line of duty. Couldn't the same happen to Stephen?

THE ONLY MAN

Her father's death and Peter's jilting had left Jennie shell-shocked and totally alone. Then her father's friend Alex Knight came to her rescue, giving her a home at his winery. But would this inscrutable man always treat her as a child—when she longed to be recognised as a woman?

TWO DIFFERENT WORLDS

Nicole was a city girl who couldn't boil an egg; Dirk Morgan was the self-sufficient wilderness expert who rescued her from a snowstorm. While they were marooned in Dirk's cabin, the attraction between them grew, but it was an attraction of opposites—so how could it last once they were back in their two different worlds?

BITTERSWEET REVENGE

BY

ROSEMARY HAMMOND

MILLS & BOON LIMITED
ETON HOUSE 18-24 PARADISE ROAD
RICHMOND SURREY TW9 1SR

First published in Great Britain 1990
by Mills & Boon Limited

This edition 1990

ISBN 0 263 76831 7

Set in Times Roman 10½ on 12 pt.
01-9010-51657 C

Made and printed in Great Britain

CHAPTER ONE

IT WAS a blistering hot day in early August. Val stood beside the open graveside in the small cemetery where her parents were buried, listening to the unfamiliar new minister give the last eulogy for David Prescott.

Bonnie and Jack Thompson were next to her, giving her moral support, and all their old schoolfriends had gathered to pay their last respects to the young man who had died so tragically just two days ago.

What a waste! Val thought as she listened to the prayers with only half an ear. Bonnie and Jack had both reassured her over and over again that she wasn't to blame in any way for David's death, that he'd always been self-destructive, and this terrible accident was only the final chapter in a long history of weakness. Although she believed them with her mind, in her heart she still felt somewhat responsible.

She glanced across the way at David's mother, a frail, grey-haired woman, dressed in black, her heavy veil pulled back. She was leaning on the arm of a tall dark man who stood beside her, grim-faced, staring blankly down at the open grave. Val knew she'd have to speak to her after the ceremony and she dreaded it.

She still couldn't quite take it in that David was gone, and as the minister droned on her thoughts wandered back to the night of the reunion party, and she replayed once again the scenario that had haunted her ever since.

* * *

The orchestra was playing its last set. Couples had already started to leave, and only a few stragglers remained out on the dance-floor. The lights were turned down low in the large banquet hall of the popular restaurant, and up above, high across the ceiling, the purple and gold cloth banner was sagging: 'Carleton High School—Ten Years.'

Val sat alone at the table listening to the tunes that had been popular ten years ago, and watching the remaining dancers. After their long conversation, David had excused himself to dance with Myra Barnes, and Val was glad of the time alone.

Their meeting had gone far better than she'd expected. In fact, spotting his dark head bent low towards Myra's, his cheek pressed against hers, she smiled to herself with satisfaction. He didn't look in the least upset. The trip back to Carleton had been well worth it. The ghosts of the past had finally been laid to rest.

Just then Bonnie came back from the powder-room and, with a weary sigh, sank into the chair next to her.

'Are you about ready to leave?' she asked. 'I'm dead beat, and we promised the sitter we'd be home by one o'clock.'

Val smiled at her old friend. 'Any time you are. Remember the days when we could go on like this all night?'

Bonnie groaned. 'What a difference ten years make to one's stamina!' She glanced around. 'Jack should be right along, then we can go.' She leaned a little closer to Val and pitched her voice low. 'Well, how did it go with David?'

'Quite well, as a matter of fact,' Val replied. 'We gave the past a good airing, and he really seemed to understand just why I left Carleton when I did, the way I did. I can't tell you what a relief that is to me. Hardly a day has gone by in the past ten years that I didn't think about it. And feel guilty.'

'Well, it wasn't your fault, after all,' Bonnie declared stoutly. 'You didn't make him into a drunk. He did that all by himself.'

'No,' Val replied with a rueful smile. 'But I didn't help him, either.'

'For God's sake, Val, you had your own plate full at the time, with your parents' death. You were only eighteen, hardly able to handle your own problems, much less David Prescott's.'

'He seems to be all right now,' Val said. 'He told me he's quit drinking, found a job and is beginning to put his life back together again. I hope so.'

Bonnie didn't say anything for a few minutes, although she looked as though she were dying to. When the orchestra finished one tune and started another, she turned to Val.

'So,' she said at last, 'what's next?'

Val gave her a puzzled look. 'What do you mean?'

'Well, where do you and David go from here? I mean, it's great that you've resolved the old bitterness, but I had the distinct impression that the main reason he wrote to ask you to come to the reunion was that he hoped to start things up with you again.'

Val widened her eyes. 'Oh, no. That isn't possible. That's all over.'

'You told him that?'

'Well, yes. What else could I do? It's the truth.'

Bonnie shook her head. 'You two seemed to be so much in love in the old days. I guess I thought you might make it work again.'

Val shook her head firmly. 'We were children,' she said. 'It's way too late, too much water under the bridge.'

'And how did David take it?'

'I already told you. He was very understanding.' Val laughed and nodded towards the dance-floor. 'As you can see by the way he and Myra are wrapped around each other, he's not pining over me.'

Suddenly Bonnie jumped to her feet and started waving. 'Here comes Jack. Now we can leave.'

Then, in the middle of that same night, had come the call from Bonnie. Val was in her hotel room, sound asleep, when the ringing of the telephone beside her bed woke her up. Groping in the darkness, she reached out for it and muttered a groggy hello.

'Val,' came Bonnie's hushed voice. 'Are you awake?'

Val struggled to a half-sitting position. 'Obviously,' she retorted drily. 'What in the world——?'

'Listen, I have some terrible news. We just heard that David Prescott was killed tonight.'

As the sudden shock-wave jolted through her, Val sat bolt upright in bed. 'What? What are you saying?'

'It's David. He was driving Myra home on the coast road. Apparently he lost control of the car, and ran off into a ditch. The car turned over, and he was killed instantly.'

'He's dead?' Val couldn't quite take it in. It was as though a part of her own childhood had suddenly been obliterated. 'How could such a thing happen?' she asked.

'Val, he was drunk,' came the curt reply.

'But he said just tonight . . .'

'I know what he said. And I'm sure he believed it at the time. But that's what the police told Jack when they called him to come and identify the body. They didn't want to upset David's mother until they were sure.'

Once she took in the stark fact that David really was gone, Val's immediate thought was that she was to blame. Once again, she'd let him down, and now this terrible thing had happened. As though reading her mind, Bonnie raised her voice in a scolding tone.

'Now, it is *not* your fault, Val. If you've got any ideas that you're to blame, put them out of your mind right now. I don't blame you in any way, and neither does Jack, who after all was his best friend. His *only* friend, I might add, for the past several years.' She paused. 'Are you OK? I'm going to send Jack over there to get you the minute he gets home from the police station.'

'No,' Val said hurriedly. 'Don't do that. I'm fine. I just need a little time. Please, don't bother Jack. He'll have enough to contend with if he has to be the one to tell David's mother. I'll be all right.'

'Well, I hope you're not going to let this spoil your whole vacation.'

'We'll see.'

The graveside ceremony was finally over, and the crowd started to break up into small groups, forming a loose line. Val had hardly dared look at David's mother during the funeral, and she steeled herself for the ordeal ahead. She'd have to offer her condolences. There was no way out of it.

She turned to Bonnie. 'I dread having to speak to Mrs Prescott.' She shivered, even though the hot August sun was beating mercilessly down on them. 'But I guess it has to be done.'

Bonnie put a hand on her arm. 'Now, don't start that again,' she warned in a stern voice. 'David's mother is a sensible woman and was well aware of his problems. She has never held you or anyone else responsible for them.' She tugged at her arm. 'Come on. Let's get it over with.'

As they took their place at the end of the dwindling line of people waiting to pay their respects, Val took a closer look at the tall man who was still at Mrs Prescott's side. She nudged Bonnie.

'Who is that man with her?'

'Oh, you remember Michael, don't you?' Bonnie asked in some surprise. 'David's older brother. He was several years ahead of us in school and wasn't around much when we were growing up. Apparently he's become quite a well-known doctor, a cardiologist, I think, somewhere in Southern California.'

Then it all came back. Michael Prescott, David's big brother, a shadowy figure who was so much older than David, at least ten years, that he was never a part of their self-absorbed crowd. She did recall vaguely hearing David speak about him, but always in a wry, almost bitter tone, as though he'd harboured some secret resentment towards him.

They were the last in line. Jack and Bonnie went on ahead and were speaking in hushed tones to Mrs Prescott, while Val hung back, waiting her turn. Then, suddenly, Bonnie turned to her, took her hand, and pulled her forward.

'Mrs Prescott, you remember Val, don't you?' she said. 'Valerie Cochran. She and David were close friends. She's living in Seattle now and came to Carleton for the reunion.'

Bonnie and Jack started walking away, leaving them alone, and Val stood there, tongue-tied, not knowing how to begin. The small grey-haired woman peered intently up at her, searching her face. Then she gave her a shaky smile and held out a black-gloved hand.

'Of course I remember you, Valerie,' she said softly. 'How could I forget? You and David were inseparable when you were children.'

Val took her hand. 'I'm so dreadfully sorry about David, Mrs Prescott,' she murmured. 'I wish——' She broke off, unable to go on.

Mrs Prescott squeezed her hand reassuringly. 'It's no one's fault, my dear,' she said sadly. 'David was my responsibility, after all, and I failed him.'

'That's nonsense, Mother,' came the low, angry voice of the man standing beside her. 'If anyone is to blame——' He broke off with an impatient gesture, then added in a softer tone, 'It's certainly not you.'

Startled, Val looked up at him, and found herself staring into the coldest pair of eyes she'd ever seen. They were the clear bright blue of an icy mountain lake, and the look of contempt and loathing on his lean, tanned face was open, unmistakable.

Now of course she did recognise him, even remembered him quite clearly as a rather remote and awesome presence who appeared at the Prescott house only on rare occasions. In fact, physically he was very much like David. Only this man was a presence, an exaggerated version of his amiable, feckless younger brother.

The black hair was coarser and thicker, glinting almost blue in the bright sun. The startling eyes were brighter, with none of David's softness, and the hard lines that ran down his cheeks along the square jaw hadn't been put there by mere age difference.

She recalled too that, by the time David was in high school, Michael had finished his medical studies and his internship and residency at a famous Los Angeles hospital, and, except for occasional short visits home, had been living away from Carleton for several years.

He was still watching her. She didn't know how to respond to his implicit accusation, and it was his mother who came to her rescue.

She gave her tall son one sharp look, then turned back to Val. 'You meant a lot to David, my dear,' she said kindly. 'But he chose his own course. I try to remember that myself.' She hesitated for a moment, then said, 'Will you be long in Carleton?'

'I had planned to spend another two weeks here,' Val replied. 'Now, I'm not so sure...' Her voice trailed off.

'If you do decide to stay, please come to see me. I'd like very much to talk to you.'

'All right. Thank you, I will. If I stay.'

With a last, muted goodbye, Val turned and walked slowly over to the kerb, where Bonnie and Jack were waiting for her in their car, obviously anxious to get home to their two small children. She climbed in the back seat and shut the door behind her without another glance back at the mother and son still standing by the graveside.

Bonnie twisted around and made a face. 'Thank God that's over with!' she said with a sigh of relief. 'I hate funerals.'

Jack started the car, and as they pulled away from the kerb he glanced at his wife. 'Where to?'

'You're coming home with us, aren't you, Val?' Bonnie asked.

'No, I don't think so,' Val replied after a moment's thought. 'As a matter of fact, I've pretty much decided to leave today.'

'Leave!' Bonnie exclaimed. 'You mean go back to Seattle?' Val nodded. 'But you still have two weeks of your vacation left!' came the vehement protest.

'Well, yes, but in the circumstances I really don't feel much like staying.' She shrugged. 'It hasn't been a very happy reunion, the way things have turned out.'

'But I was counting on having a real visit with you,' Bonnie went on. 'You've only been here a few days, not even a week, and with all the fuss over preparing for the reunion party we haven't had time for one good talk.' She turned to her husband. 'Jack, tell her she has to stay.'

Jack Thompson was a quiet man who taught science at the high school they'd all attended. Although he kept a tight discipline in his classes, he'd long deferred personal decisions to his more ebullient wife and wasn't about to tell Val what to do.

'Well, Bonnie,' he said mildly, 'Val has to do what she thinks is best.' He raised his head and met Val's eyes in the rear-view mirror. 'But I don't see any reason why you shouldn't finish up your vacation here. It's been a long time.'

'And we had lots of things planned!' Bonnie said accusingly. 'Who knows when you'll get back down here again? Come on, Val, say you'll stay.'

Val smiled. 'All right, but not the whole two weeks. Maybe a few more days.'

Jack had reached the main intersection and came to a stop at the sign. 'In the meantime,' he said patiently, 'where to?'

'Back to the hotel, please, Jack,' Val said quickly and firmly before Bonnie could chime in with an order of her own. 'I have some things I need to take care of.'

'But you're still coming for dinner tonight, aren't you?' Bonnie asked.

'Yes, of course.'

'Good. I'll send Jack to pick you up around six o'clock.'

'No, don't bother,' Val said hurriedly. 'As long as I'm going to stay a while longer, I think I'll rent a car.'

Bonnie opened her mouth, but even she knew when Val really meant it, so she only nodded and turned to her husband. 'I guess it's the hotel, Jack.'

On the way to Val's hotel—the one hotel the small town of Carleton boasted—they were all too subdued by the sombre graveside ceremony to make much conversation. When they dropped Val off, she got out quickly, anxious to be alone.

When she let herself into her room, the first thing that caught her eye, still sitting on the dresser where she'd left it, was David's letter. It was what had brought her back to the town she'd grown up in after ten years away from it.

She went slowly, almost fearfully, over to the dresser, picked up the letter and read it again. 'Dear Val,' it said. 'As you know by now, we're planning our tenth high school reunion party next month. I'm writing to ask you to please come. You and I have some unfinished business to discuss. I know I blamed you for what happened, but I'm slowly getting my act together again, and it would mean a lot to me to see you again, get the past resolved, once and for all. Perhaps even make a new beginning.'

When she'd received the letter at her apartment in Seattle a month ago, her first impulse had been that of course she couldn't possibly go. She'd left Carleton so precipitately, and under such a cloud, with so many hard feelings, that she'd vowed never to return.

In the end, however, she'd decided to go after all. She had vacation time coming from the exclusive boutique where she worked as principal buyer. It must have taken a lot of courage for David to write that letter. And she hadn't exaggerated when she'd told Bonnie she'd carried around a burden of guilt for ten long years. It would give her a chance to lay the past to rest, to heal old wounds.

And that was exactly what it had done. If David had actually harboured any hopes of resuming their childhood romance, as Bonnie suspected and as the letter hinted, he had taken it quite well when she'd told him kindly but firmly that there was no chance of that ever happening.

He'd protested, tried to convince her to give it another try, but only mildly, and it hadn't taken that much to persuade him she meant it, that it had nothing to do with him, that romance had no place in her life. Not with anyone. He certainly hadn't seemed heart-broken at the time. What had happened later was *not* her fault.

She folded up the letter and put it in her handbag, then just before she turned away she caught a glimpse of her reflection in the mirror over the dresser. She put a hand on her face, frowning. Where had all the softness gone? Somehow, being back in Carleton, she'd expected to see the image of the eighteen-year-old girl she'd been when she left.

The streaky brown hair was the same, just as shiny, with the same blonde highlights, but severely drawn back now instead of hanging in loose waves to her shoulders. Her posture was stiffer, too, and she shook her shoulders in an effort to loosen the tense muscles.

Most of all, though, the inward change showed in her eyes. The hazel that used to be alight with the sheer joy of living now seemed glazed over permanently with a hard, protective veneer of reserve and suspicion.

She turned quickly away from the mirror and went over to lie down on the bed. Before long, just a few more days, and she'd be back in Seattle, her own apartment, her wonderful job. It was good that she had come, but it would be even better to return to her real life.

The next afternoon, without having consciously made the decision, Val found herself driving along the country road north of town that led to the old Prescott house.

She'd started out after lunch at Bonnie's with the idea of taking a short drive to visit some of her old familiar haunts, and she wanted to do it alone. She'd spent last evening and most of the morning with Bonnie, catching up on their lives, and when she'd announced her plan Bonnie hadn't objected. The children had been fretful all morning anyway, and she'd almost seemed to welcome a chance to get them settled down.

On the short drive, Val had passed by her own old home, the schools she had attended, the tennis-courts where she'd spent so many happy hours with David, the soda fountain that had been their crowd's favourite hang-out.

Each spot brought back a flood of memories, some pleasant, some painful, and it almost seemed as though she had never left the town, never picked up and flown to her grandmother's house in Seattle after her parents' sudden death.

She still shuddered at the memory of that awful day, the arrival of the police bringing her the news that both her mother and father had been killed in a car accident, finding out later that her father had been driving while intoxicated, then the hysterical telephone call to her grandmother, the hasty flight to Seattle.

It had all happened so fast that her head had spun for weeks. She had often wondered through the years if she couldn't somehow have done things differently, if there hadn't been a better way to handle the situation. Now, especially with David dead, she regretted her hasty actions even more deeply, and wished she'd had the maturity to treat him more considerately.

They had been a pair for so long, best friends since early childhood, then sweethearts during adolescence. It had been very wrong of her to just leave the way she did with only a letter for explanation. At the time, stunned by the sudden loss of both parents, seeing David heading in the same direction as her father, all she had been able to think of was to get as far away as possible.

Then, suddenly, she knew why her apparently aimless drive had brought her to the Prescott house.

When she was eighteen, she'd left town with unfinished business that had haunted her for ten years. She didn't want to make the same mistake again. She had to make her peace with David's memory once and for all before she could leave this time.

The house was set at the top of a gentle rise, that sloped up from the narrow road to the right. Val turned in at the open gate and headed up the winding driveway that led to the front of the house. There was no other car in sight.

She parked and went up the wide wooden steps to the front door of the house, which was almost as familiar as her own. She and David had been inseparable in those days, in and out of each other's homes almost every day. Everything looked exactly the same, even to the lace curtains at the windows, the two clay urns of geraniums set on either side of the door, the sweet scent of the tall acacia tree overhanging the weather-beaten porch.

She took a deep breath, raised her hand and knocked. After a few moments, she heard slow footsteps coming from inside, then the door opened and Mrs Prescott, still dressed in black, appeared at the other side, peering up at her.

'Valerie!' she said in some surprise. Then she smiled. 'Please come in.'

As Val crossed the threshold, she felt as though she were stepping back into her own past. She looked up at the winding staircase, half expecting David to come bounding down to greet her as he used to.

'Come into the kitchen,' Mrs Prescott was saying. 'We'll have a cup of tea.'

Val followed her into the large country kitchen. The same refrigerator and stove sat side by side on one wall, and, although the cupboards had recently been painted, they were still the same bright yellow colour. In the middle of the floor was the same round table, covered with a pale green cotton cloth.

'I'm so glad you decided to come,' the older woman said. 'Sit down, and I'll just put the water on to boil.'

'I hope this isn't an inconvenient time to visit,' Val said as she seated herself at the table. 'I'll only be in Carleton for another day or two, and I didn't want to go before seeing you.'

Mrs Prescott set the kettle on the fire, then sat down across from Val. 'It's a perfect time,' she said warmly. 'And I'm grateful you decided to come. I've thought so often of the old days, when you were here with David. I almost thought of you as one of my own children.' She hesitated, then added, 'And I think you know I always hoped you would be one day.'

'Mrs Prescott,' Val said helplessly, 'I'd like to explain to you about that if I can. I know how wrong I was, how much I hurt David by the way I left Carleton, but at the time I was so confused and frightened I didn't know what else to do.'

'You don't have to explain anything to me, Valerie,' she said firmly. 'I told you that yesterday. No one knew David's weaknesses better than I. You didn't cause his problems, and there was nothing you could have done to cure them.'

'Perhaps not,' Val agreed reluctantly. 'But the fact remains that I did hurt him badly.' She leaned forward and gazed earnestly into the other woman's eyes. 'I was so afraid,' she said, her voice barely audible. 'After the way my father was, when I saw David getting worse, drinking more, refusing to listen to me, I simply realised there was no future for us. Then, when my parents were killed in that awful way, I didn't even feel I *had* a future.' She spread her hands helplessly. 'So I just ran.'

'All I can do, Valerie, is assure you that I do understand, and I don't blame you in any way. And you mustn't ever blame yourself.'

The kettle began to sing, and Mrs Prescott got up to make the tea. As she poured it out, she spoke to Val over her shoulder. 'Now that we have that settled, tell me what you've been doing with yourself for the past ten years.' She carried the steaming cups to the table and set them down. 'As I recall, you went to live with your grandmother after your parents died.'

'Yes. She was wonderful. She died herself just a few years ago, and I still miss her. She had a little house in Seattle, with a lovely garden, and she took me in without a question.'

'And you never married?'

'No,' Val replied shortly. What she didn't say was that after what had happened with her father, then with David, the two men she'd loved most in the world, she hadn't trusted herself to get that close to any man ever again.

'Why not?'

Val shrugged non-committally. 'Well, for one thing, I've been busy. There wasn't any money for an education, so I started working in a small dress shop right away. After I learned the retail clothing business, I went on to one of the more exclusive boutiques. I have a good position there now as head buyer.'

'And you enjoy your work?'

'Oh, I love it. I travel a lot to style showings in New York and San Francisco and Chicago. Next year I plan a trip to Paris.'

'You've done very well, Valerie. You must be proud of your accomplishments.'

Val smiled. 'Well, I've been very lucky.'

There was a short silence then as the two women drank their tea. It wasn't uncomfortable, however, and as Val found herself relaxing in Mrs Prescott's kind presence she was very glad she'd come. If his own mother exonerated her from all blame for David's tragic end, then she had nothing to reproach herself with. She could go back home now with a clear conscience and a free heart.

In fact, now that this old ghost had been laid to rest, it might even be possible that there would be a more personal future in store for her. She was only twenty-eight, still young enough to marry, have a family. Her job was satisfying and secure, she'd accomplished what she had set out to do in it.

But something was missing. In spite of her success, the friends she had made, she was lonely and felt as though, in some important ways, she hadn't really begun to live.

'I've been wondering,' Mrs Prescott broke into her reverie at last, 'if you wouldn't like something of David's, some belonging to remember him by.'

It was on the tip of Val's tongue to say no, that she didn't want to be reminded of him at all, but she stopped herself in time. That wasn't the way to be free. Besides, it was a friendly gesture, and she didn't want to hurt his mother's feelings. She searched her mind, trying to jog her memory to come up with a suitable object.

'There is one thing,' she said slowly. 'David and I bought each other class rings as a graduation gift.

Kind of silly, really, since they both cost the same. If you don't mind, I'd like to have David's ring.'

Mrs Prescott's face brightened. 'What a lovely idea!' she said. 'I think I know just where it is.' She rose from her chair. 'You stay right there, I won't be a minute.'

When she was gone, Val got up and walked over to the window, which overlooked the gentle sweep of the hill, the yellow acacia tree, the long curved driveway. As she gazed out at the pleasant familiar sight, she noticed a car turning into the drive from the main road. It was sleek, silvery grey, obviously an expensive model.

Another condolence caller, she thought as she watched it climb slowly towards the house. It was time for her to leave anyway. As soon as Mrs Prescott came back with David's ring, she'd make her excuses and go. She'd accomplished what she'd set out to do, made her peace with David's mother as well as his memory. She was free at last of the past.

By now, the car had parked behind hers, and she was just about to go back to the table to gather up her handbag when the driver's door opened and a man got out. She drew in her breath sharply and stared, rooted to the spot. It was David's brother, Michael! She'd assumed he had gone back to Los Angeles after the funeral yesterday. If she'd known he'd be here, she would never have come. The hostility in his tone in those few short words he'd spoken to her then had been unmistakable.

It was too late now. He was already on the porch. She'd just have to face him and get out as quickly and gracefully as she could. She went back to the table and picked up her handbag, then stood there waiting, her heart pounding, as the front door opened and closed and his footsteps came down the hall towards the kitchen.

When he appeared in the doorway and saw her standing there, he stopped short. A hard glint appeared in the bright blue eyes, and the corners of his mouth turned down in a frown.

'Hello, Michael,' she said stiffly.

He didn't utter a word, just continued to stand there staring at her. Val had the distinct impression, just from the way he held himself, the way he looked at her, that he wanted nothing more than to march over to her and wipe her off the face of the earth, and she instinctively backed away from him a step.

Finally he spoke. 'Just what the hell are you doing here?' he asked in a low voice.

CHAPTER TWO

VAL clutched her handbag to her chest. 'I was just leaving,' she said. 'And I came to see your mother because she asked me to.'

He looked past her, still frowning, his hands in his trouser pockets, jingling keys and change. He was dressed casually in a pair of clean tan chinos and a blue knitted shirt, open at the throat, and which exactly matched the colour of his piercing blue eyes.

Although his shoulders were broad and his muscular structure taut and well-knit, he didn't have an athlete's massive build. But there was a sense of enormous reserves of power in him, whether physical, emotional or mental, and the thought struck Val that he would be a formidable opponent in any contest.

He crossed over to the kitchen counter, turned around and leaned his narrow hips back against it, his arms folded across his chest. Once again she was struck by the resemblance to David, as well as the differences. He had exactly the same colouring, even the same slim build, but in this man there was the hint of strong emotion, even anger, barely contained beneath a surface reserve. And right now it seemed to be directed at her.

He eyed her narrowly. 'I'm surprised you had the nerve to come here,' he said in a flat, toneless voice.

Val raised her chin. 'I told you,' she said defiantly. 'Your mother invited me. It *is* her house.'

When he made no reply and merely continued to stare at her as though she were some species of loathsome insect, Val suddenly saw red. David's mother had absolved her of any guilt, and that was all she needed. This man had no right to accuse her of anything. As her anger escalated, she found herself gradually beginning to make her way across the room towards him, until finally she stopped not two feet away from where he stood.

She clenched her fists at her sides and looked up at him with fire in her eyes. 'If you have something to say to me, Michael,' she said tersely, 'then you'd better come right out with it and get it off your chest before it chokes you.'

He pushed himself away from the counter, covering the distance between them, and stood looming over her. 'All right,' he snapped. 'I will. To begin with, I think we both know quite well what was at the bottom of David's problems.'

'Yes,' she retorted. 'We do. It was his own weakness. Your own mother says so.'

He raised one heavy black eyebrow. 'You may have fooled my mother into believing that innocent act of yours, but you'll find that I'm not quite so gullible.'

'All right, then, if you have all the answers, perhaps you'd better tell me what they are.'

'I intend to,' he said smoothly. He raised a hand and began ticking off on his fingers. 'To begin with, you led him on all the time you were both growing up. He was utterly convinced that you really cared about him, that you were destined to be together. Every time I came home he was full of nothing but you, how much he cared for you, how you planned on marrying when you finished school.'

'But I *did* care,' she said. 'I believed all that, too.'

He brushed that off with an impatient gesture and gave a harsh laugh. 'God, he even asked me for advice, and, fool that I was, I encouraged him, told him how rare that kind of closeness was, even that I envied him.'

She opened her mouth to ask him what business he had giving his brother advice when he was gone so much he hardly knew him, but he already had a hand held up to stop her before she could get the first word out.

What good would it do anyway? She might as well hear him out, let him get it off his chest, then she could leave. She *wished* his mother would come back!

'Second,' he went on, 'when you decided he was too much for you to handle, you simply left town, without even giving him a chance to stop you. He showed me the letter you wrote him. Very comforting *that* little gem was for a kid whose heart was breaking.'

'And do you have any idea what I was going through then?' she asked in a voice throbbing with emotion. 'I could barely keep from falling apart myself after my mother and father were killed. How could I help him? I was only eighteen years old!'

He gave her a curt nod. 'All right,' he said grudgingly. 'I'll grant you that. In fact, your leaving was probably the best thing you could have done for him. He had a rough time getting over you, but after literally years of self-destructive behaviour he was finally getting his life together. And then——' He pounded his fist in his other hand. '*Then* you have to show up again!'

'I came back because David himself wrote and begged me to,' she shouted. Fed up by now with the inquisition, she thrust her face up close to his. 'Just what gives you the right to question my actions? Where were you when David started drinking? Why didn't you do something about it when you saw him falling to pieces?'

As their eyes locked together in a silent battle of wills that threatened to erupt into violence at any second, it suddenly struck Val that behind the hard veneer was real pain. Her gaze faltered, her anger began to leak away, and she lifted her hand in a helpless gesture.

'Michael,' she said wearily, 'I know how hard losing David has been for you. And you might be right. Perhaps I am partly to blame for what happened to him. But was it fair to expect me to save him from himself? To have manufactured a love I simply didn't feel any more?'

'No!' he snapped. 'Of course not. If, indeed, you're capable of love, no one expected you to give it to David just because he needed it. I'm not even saying that would have solved his problems.' He clenched his jaw and the blue eyes burned into hers. 'But why the hell did you have to come back?' he ground out.

To her amazement, she saw the glitter of tears in his eyes. A wave of pity for him swept over her, and she felt her own unshed tears rising to the surface. She wanted to reach out to him, to help him in some way. But before she could make a move or utter a word, he had turned away from her with a muttered curse.

At this absolute rejection, she simply lost it. Choking and sobbing, she covered her face with her hands, whirled around and rushed blindly towards the door.

Then she heard Mrs Prescott's voice, surprisingly strong for such a frail woman. 'Michael, what have you done? Stop it this instant!'

She put an arm around Val's heaving shoulders and led her out into the hall. By the time they reached the front door, Val had collected herself enough to get a handkerchief out of her bag, dry her eyes and wipe her nose.

Mrs Prescott gave her a sympathetic pat. 'My dear, I'm so sorry. Please forgive my son. He feels David's death terribly. He'd never admit it, but I think deep down he believes he failed his brother.' She smiled wryly. 'Although he's not the kind of man who likes to face such unpleasant truths about himself.'

'I'm sorry, too,' Val said with a sigh. 'I probably shouldn't have come. And I wouldn't have if I'd known Michael would still be here. He made it quite clear how he felt about me at the funeral.'

'Nonsense! I'm very grateful to you for coming. Michael is——' She broke off with a shrug. 'Well, just Michael, a strong man, but with his own weaknesses, just like anyone else. In any case, he does plan to leave in a day or two. If you're going to be in town for a while, I'd like to see you again.'

'I really don't know what my plans are at this point,' Val said. She smiled weakly. 'I think it would probably be best for all concerned if I left as soon as possible.'

Mrs Prescott held out her hand, palm up to reveal David's ring. 'Here. I do want you to have this.'

As Val stared down at the ring that she had given to David so long ago, she was surprised at how little power it had to move her. She really had loved him then, but now all she felt was a terrible sadness at the tragic waste.

'Thank you,' she said, putting the ring into her bag. 'Now I'd better go.'

She opened the door and stepped out on to the porch. The scent of the acacia blossoms was heavy in the hot, sultry afternoon air and in the tall grass insects were buzzing. The house had been so dim and cool that she blinked at the bright sunshine still beating down. The car would be stifling.

'Goodbye, then,' Mrs Prescott said. 'And I do hope you'll decide to stay a while longer, for your own sake. You should make sure that your unfinished business really is taken care of this time.'

As Val drove back towards town along the familiar streets, she pondered those parting words. When she had first arrived at the Prescott house, not two hours ago, she had honestly believed the old ghosts were all laid to rest.

Now, still shaken in the aftermath of the ugly scene with Michael, she wasn't so sure. If she hadn't already promised Bonnie to stay a while longer, she'd make tracks for Seattle as fast as she could, and leave the muddied past behind forever.

Right now, however, she was due at Bonnie's house. Although the last thing she wanted was the good heart-to-heart conversation they'd planned, she knew she couldn't disappoint her old friend, and when she reached their street she automatically turned into the Thompson driveway.

She had just parked the car in front and switched off the engine when Bonnie herself came bustling down the path to meet her. At the sight of her round plump face, wreathed in a glad smile of anticipation, Val was glad she'd come. It would do her good, and might even help her get the bad taste of that encounter with Michael Prescott out of her mouth.

'You'll never guess!' Bonnie exclaimed. 'Jack took the kids out to Marsh Creek for a picnic, which means we have a chance for a good visit by ourselves. They've been absolute monsters for the past few days. I only hope they're not coming down with something.'

'I meant to get here sooner,' Val said as she followed Bonnie into the small, cosy living-room. 'But I took a drive and ended up at the Prescott place.'

Bonnie only raised an enquiring eyebrow, but after she'd settled herself beside Val on the couch and poured out the iced tea she turned to her with a decidedly curious glint in her eye.

'Well, how did that go?'

Val took a grateful cooling swallow of tea. 'Not too well,' she said wryly. 'Michael was there.'

Bonnie rolled her eyes. 'Oh, oh. Sounds sticky.'

'I don't know, Bonnie. Maybe he's right in blaming me for what happened to David.'

'Stop that!' Bonnie ordered sternly. 'We've been all over the subject, and I thought we'd agreed to drop it for good. If you ask me, Michael Prescott is taking his own guilt out on you.'

Val gave her a sharp look. 'The thought did cross my mind,' she said slowly. 'But I don't want to kid myself. It's just as unfair to blame him, I guess, as it is anyone else.'

'True,' Bonnie agreed. 'But that doesn't alter the fact that he has no business putting the whole thing off on you.' She shook her fair, untidy curls. 'He was always hard to figure out, something of a mystery man, actually, if you recall. Maybe it was just because he was so much older than David's crowd. More like his uncle—or even his father—than his brother.'

'Poor David never did have a father, did he? He was just a baby when he died. It might have made all the difference if he'd lived. I wonder what he was like.'

Bonnie snorted. 'If Michael is any indication, I visualise him as stern, arrogant and very, very superior.'

Val laughed. 'Is that how you see Michael?'

She recalled the tears she'd seen in his eyes that afternoon. Somewhere beneath that hard exterior was a vast reservoir of emotion, and she wondered idly if any woman had ever tapped into it.

'Well, if the shoe fits,' Bonnie proclaimed loftily. She reached out for the plate of sandwiches. 'You'll have to admit, though, that in spite of his unpleasant personality he's a very attractive man.'

'Yes, I suppose so,' Val murmured. She took a cucumber sandwich and bit into it. 'Is he married, I wonder?'

Bonnie shook her head vigorously. 'Heavens, no! From what I hear, he's been too busy making a big name for himself in medicine. Jack tells me he's a cardiologist, by the way. Actually, a cardiac surgeon, but heavily into research at some foundation in Los Angeles.' She batted her eyelids suggestively. 'Although gossip has it that his commitment to his work hasn't stopped him from indulging in some very interesting dalliance.'

'Dalliance!' Val sputtered, half choking on her sandwich. 'What does that mean?'

'It means, my dear,' Bonnie drawled, 'that his name has been linked from time to time with an heiress, a movie star and lord knows what else. In other words, the "love 'em and leave 'em" type.' She settled back on the couch. 'But enough of Michael Prescott. I want to hear about you. Your letters give me the facts, but they don't tell me what's really been going on in your life.'

'I'm afraid that, actually, they do,' Val responded with a little laugh. 'My job is pretty much all I have time for.'

'No romance?'

Val shook her head. It was a subject she wasn't comfortable discussing. 'Nothing worth mentioning, anyway,' she replied.

Adroitly changing the subject, she asked Bonnie about her children, and when her friend immediately brightened and launched into a long description of their accomplishments she settled back to listen attentively with an inward sigh of relief.

It was past four o'clock before she got up to go, almost time for Jack to return with the children. The plan was for the three of them to go out to dinner that night, and Val was looking forward to a nice quiet rest first in her room at the hotel. The whole day had been one long drain on her emotional resources.

'I'll be back around seven,' she promised at the door. 'And tonight it's to be my treat. Will you have any problem getting a sitter for the children?'

'No, that's all taken care of,' Bonnie replied.

Val was just about to turn to go when a thought struck her. 'Say, Bonnie, have you heard anything about how Myra Barnes is doing? She must have been badly hurt in the accident.'

Bonnie nodded. 'Yes, several broken bones and a concussion. Luckily—or unluckily for David—the impact was on the driver's side, so at least she wasn't killed.'

'Have you been to the hospital to see her?'

'No,' Bonnie said, 'and I feel a little guilty about it. I've been so harried trying to keep those fussy kids amused that I haven't had the time. I always liked Myra, too, even if she is a little scatter-brained.'

'Yes,' Val said slowly. 'I did, too. As long as I'm going to stick around for a few more days, maybe I'll go see her myself.'

Some time later Val woke up with a jolt out of a sound sleep. Before lying down, she had closed the curtains, and the room was so dim she couldn't even guess at the time. She glanced at her watch. It was already six-thirty and she was due at the Thompsons' at seven.

She had just swung her legs over the bed when the telephone rang. It was Bonnie, and she sounded on the edge of panic.

'The children are both terribly sick,' she said in a rush. 'It looks ominously like measles, according to the doctor. I'm afraid our dinner date is off.'

'Of course,' Val assured her. 'No problem. And try not to worry. All children get measles, don't they? I'll call you tomorrow to see how they are.'

After she hung up, she walked slowly into the bathroom. She was a little disappointed that the dinner was cancelled, but in a way relieved. It would be pleasant to have a meal alone in the hotel dining-room. Ever since she'd arrived in Carleton, each day had been filled with activity of some kind, and she really hadn't had a chance to gather her wits since the accident.

The long nap had done her a world of good, and as she lay soaking in the hot tub it almost seemed as though the whole series of events since the night of the reunion party was fading into a bad dream. She might even finish her whole two weeks in Carleton as planned. She could look up some of her other old friends, especially now that Bonnie was apparently going to be tied to sick children.

She dressed carefully in a coral-coloured linen dress. As head buyer in a fashionable boutique, she had to have a fairly extensive wardrobe herself, and was used to dressing well. She brushed her hair until it shone, the blonde highlights brighter from the California sun. Then she put on a light trace of pale lip-gloss and clipped on a pair of coral earrings that just matched the dress and she was ready to go down to dinner.

She had picked up her handbag and was just starting for the door when the telephone rang again. She frowned, hoping a little guiltily that it wasn't Bonnie again saying they could make it after all. But when she picked up the receiver and answered, a strange masculine voice was at the other end of the line.

'Valerie, this is Michael Prescott.'

Val was so taken aback that she had to think for a moment who Michael Prescott was. Then, when the image of the tall man formed in her mind, she steeled herself. What in the world could he be calling for?

'Yes?' she said curtly.

There was a short silence, then he went on in a smooth, self-confident tone. 'My mother tells me that I behaved boorishly to you this afternoon, and I thought I'd like to try to make it up to you in some way.'

Val couldn't believe her ears. 'Well, please assure your mother that there's no need for you to do anything of the kind,' she retorted.

'Well, actually, it wasn't just for her sake that I called.' The voice was still bland, insouciant. 'I think we still have a few things to talk over, and I'd like to take you out to dinner if you don't have other plans.'

She was about to make an excuse, to lie and say she had another dinner date, but at the last minute caught herself. Michael Prescott was the last person on earth she wanted to see at the moment. What would be the harm in letting him know that?

'No,' she said snappishly. 'I don't have any other plans. But I certainly don't want to have dinner with you. We have nothing to talk about. You said everything you needed to this afternoon, and I'm not in the mood to hear any more accusations.'

'Hey, wait a minute,' he said. 'It wasn't my intention to accuse you of anything or cause you any more trouble. I just wanted to talk things over with you before you left.'

'Well, I'm afraid I don't,' she said firmly. 'Thank you anyway for the most gracious invitation. I'm going to hang up now. Goodbye.'

She felt a very powerful impulse to slam the receiver down in his ear, but instead she set it down carefully in its cradle. It was then that she noticed how badly she was shaking. The conversation had disturbed her deeply, brought all the unpleasantness back into sharp focus again, just when she'd thought she was over it.

However, she was not going to allow Michael Prescott to ruin her nice quiet evening. She'd planned to have dinner alone in the dining-room, and that was just what she was going to do.

She drank a martini before dinner, then a split of California Vouvray with her chicken Kiev, and by the time her after-dinner coffee was served she felt much better.

She leaned back in her chair and scanned the room idly. The nerve of the man! Clearly he'd had the idea that all he had to do was call her up with some cock-and-bull story about wanting to 'talk things over' to send her grovelling at his feet. No one she cared about blamed her for what had happened to David, and she would not let this overbearing man make her feel guilty.

The waiter had come to hover at her elbow, and she was consulting the menu, debating between dessert and an after-dinner drink, when she happened to look up. She drew in her breath sharply when there at the entrance she saw the overbearing man himself, in the flesh.

He was making directly for her table. Was his appearance here a coincidence, or was the tracking her down? Quickly, she grabbed her handbag, ready to jump up and run out of the room before he could reach her.

Then she thought, Why should I let him drive me out? She looked up at the waiter. 'I'll have a Brandy Alexander,' she said, and when he'd gone she folded her hands in front of her on the table, stony-faced, waiting.

It was far too late to pretend she hadn't seen him anyway, so she sat and watched him as he strode towards her, his gait confident and purposeful. He was dressed in well-fitting grey trousers and a navy linen blazer. His white shirt set off his deep tan, and the blue tie was exactly the colour of his eyes.

Val gave a quick sideways glance around the room at the other diners. While it wasn't exactly crowded, there were enough other people there to give her a feeling of reassurance, even safety. Then she almost had to laugh at the ridiculous thought. Surely there was no danger that he would do her any actual bodily harm?

He stopped when he came to her table and put both his hands on the back of the chair opposite her. She raised her eyes and gave him a cool, questioning look, her mouth clamped shut, waiting for him to speak.

'May I sit down?' he asked.

She gave him a curt nod. 'Suit yourself,' she said ungraciously. 'Although,' she added as he slid into the chair, 'I still don't see that we have anything to talk about.'

The waiter appeared just then with her drink, and after he'd set it down he eyed Michael questioningly. 'Anything for you, sir?'

'Scotch and soda, please. No ice.'

When the waiter had gone, Michael leaned back in his chair and eyed Val speculatively, his expression bland, not quite smiling, but without any overt hostility, almost as though he was waiting for her to say something. Averting her eyes, she took a quick sip of her drink. They could sit there without speaking all night as far as she was concerned.

Still, the silence grew unnerving. She had the feeling he was deliberately trying to make her uncomfortable, even employing some kind of tactical manoeuvre in a game of wits. If so, he was succeeding admirably. It was all she could do to keep from squirming in her chair, and she was relieved when the waiter came back with his drink, breaking the tension momentarily.

When they were alone again, and he still didn't say anything, she decided to simply get up out of her chair and walk out on him. However, she'd barely touched her drink, and she hated to give him the satisfaction of driving her away—from *her* table.

Finally he spoke. 'You look very nice tonight,' he said smoothly. 'That colour suits you.'

She only goggled at him. It was the last thing in the world she'd expected him to say, and she had no idea how to respond. She took another quick swallow of her drink to cover her confusion, and cast around wildly in her mind for something to say.

'How did you know I'd be here?' she finally blurted out.

He shrugged. 'It wasn't hard. I knew you were staying at the hotel, and when you said you were eating alone I just took the chance you'd be in the dining-room.'

Then he smiled. It was the first time she'd seen anything even remotely resembling good will towards her on his face, and it transformed him utterly. The lines on either side of his mouth smoothed out into deeply cleft dimples, and his white, even teeth sparkled against his dark skin.

She gave him a suspicious look. 'So, clever you. You tracked me down. What for?'

'I already explained that when I called earlier.'

'Oh, yes,' she said drily. 'Your mother sent you.'

He gave her one startled look, then threw back his head and laughed openly. Val stared, transfixed, at the long column of his throat, the lift of his strong chin, the flashing blue eyes.

'Touché,' he said at last. He put his elbows on the table, holding his glass in both hands, turning it around slowly, and leaned forward, quite serious now. 'David's death was a terrible shock to me,' he said soberly. 'You were right. I probably was taking it out on you. I'd like to—well—I guess an apology is in order.'

For a moment she was tempted by an almost overwhelming urge to trust him, to believe him. He seemed sincere. He was watching her carefully, waiting for her response. She lowered her eyes.

He had set his glass down, and his hands were lying flat on top of the table. Surgeon's hands, she thought, staring at them, large, capable, with long, sensitive fingers and lightly covered with silky black hair. He wore no rings.

He was a *very* attractive man. In any other circumstances... But it was all too pat, too smooth. There hadn't been any real regret in the half-hearted apology, if that was what you could call it.

She gave him a tight smile. 'All right,' she said briskly. 'That's fair enough. Apology accepted.'

He nodded with satisfaction. 'Good,' he said with another wonderful smile.

She knew now that she had to get out of there. Much more of this cosy tête-à-tête and she would actually begin to *like* the man.

She took one last sip of her drink, not enough to drain the glass, but as close as she could manage. Then she rose abruptly to her feet.

'Now, if you'll excuse me...'

He was out of his chair instantly. 'Where are you going?'

'To my room.'

'You haven't finished your drink.'

She glanced down at his own half-empty glass. 'Neither have you,' she said.

She turned and walked away from him, her spine stiff, her shoulders back, her head high, conscious at every step of the way that the blue gaze was following her. She kept her eyes straight ahead, fighting the temptation to turn back to see if he was following her.

When she reached the lobby she marched directly around the front desk and headed for the lift, out of his line of sight at last. After punching the button, she did dare one quick glance over her shoulder. The lobby was empty.

She slouched into the waiting lift and, as the doors slowly closed behind her, she breathed a heavy sigh of relief. She'd won that round, she thought smugly, as she was borne upwards. For some obscure reason, he had decided to charm her, and she'd resisted admirably.

But as she let herself into her room she couldn't quite ward off a nagging sense of regret, even disappointment, that he had given up so easily and had not come after her. It might have been interesting to stay a while and find out just what it was he really wanted from her.

She soon realised the folly of *that* line of reasoning. Granted, he was probably the most attractive man she'd ever met, but she'd known lots of good-looking men, and every one of them had been so in love with himself that the only part a woman had played in his life was an admiring audience. And even though

Michael did seem to have warmed slightly towards her, she still sensed real danger in him.

It was then that it occurred to her that not once, even when he'd smiled or laughed in apparently genuine amusement, had any hint of warmth softened the cold glint of those icy blue eyes.

CHAPTER THREE

BY MORNING, Val had successfully banished all thoughts of Michael Prescott from her mind. She was glad he'd come to make his peace with her last night and that they hadn't parted enemies, but his mother had said he was leaving town soon. She would most likely never see him again.

She called Bonnie right after breakfast, as she'd promised, to learn that both children were in bed with high fevers, and it would be days before she could leave them.

'So will you please stay in town a while longer?' she begged. 'Otherwise I won't even get a chance to see you again. It's definitely measles.'

'I'll think about it,' Val said with a sigh, and they hung up without any definite promises being made.

The trouble was, she had no idea what to do with herself if she did stay much longer. She supposed she could look up some of her other high-school friends, but during the ten years she'd been away they'd drifted apart and would have little in common. Besides that, most of them were married, and in Val's experience women with husbands tended to disappear as friends.

The main reason she'd come to Carleton was to tend to unfinished business. David's death had put the seal of finality on their relationship, and in her heart she believed he had forgiven her in the end. So had his mother. Even his hostile brother had offered a grudging olive-branch last night. She felt she was free of the past at last.

With her business finished in Carleton, she might as well go back to Seattle. She had friends there she could spend some time with. She could catch up on her reading, maybe spend a day or two at the ocean. She'd been planning to paint the apartment. Now might be a good time.

Then she remembered that she'd half decided to go to the hospital to visit Myra Barnes, the girl who had been with David the night of the accident. They hadn't been close friends in school, as she and Bonnie had, but they'd travelled in the same circles, and it would be an act of kindness to go and see her. It couldn't be much fun to be confined to a hospital bed on a fine summer day, with broken bones and a concussion.

She called the hospital and was told that Myra was resting as comfortably as could be expected with casts on both legs and in traction, but that she was able to receive visitors.

It was another scorching hot August day, the sun beating down mercilessly on the parched brown hills. Val had worn a pale yellow cotton sun-dress with a halter-top, but even so just the short walk from the car park to the entrance of the small local hospital had brought out beads of perspiration on her face and arms.

Inside, she was greeted with a blast of blessedly cool air-conditioning. At the desk, she was directed to a room on the second floor, and when she got there she could hear the low murmur of voices coming through the open door.

She hesitated, not wanting to intrude. However, she had stopped along the way to pick up a small bouquet of flowers, a cheerful arrangement of white daisies and yellow roses in a round glass bowl, and she had to do something with it.

She rapped lightly on the door, pushed it open and stepped inside. There was only one bed in the room, with a white screen around it. Perhaps she was having a bath, or being examined. Val walked hesitantly over to the screen, then stopped.

'Myra,' she called softly. 'It's Val Cochran. Is this a bad time for a visit?'

The screen was pushed aside then, and the tall form of Michael Prescott was revealed. Val stood there, the vase of flowers in her hand, staring. What in the world was he doing here? He was the last person she would have expected to see.

He flashed her a wry smile. 'So, we meet again.'

'So we do,' Val murmured. Then she glanced at the figure lying on the bed. 'Hello, Myra,' she said. 'How are you feeling?'

'Val?' Myra asked. 'Val Cochran? What a nice surprise!'

'It looks as though you already have company,' Val said, with a glance at Michael. 'I can come back later.'

'I was just leaving,' he said. He turned to the girl in the bed. 'You seem to be in good hands here, Myra,' he said softly, 'and making excellent progress. In six weeks or so those bones will knit and you'll be as good as new.'

'Thank you for coming, Michael,' Myra said. 'Will I see you again?'

Michael darted a swift sideways glance at Val, one heavy dark eyebrow raised, almost as though asking her a question. Then he turned back to Myra and took her hand.

'I'm not sure what my plans are,' he said. 'If I do stay in town a while longer, I'll be back. You can count on it.'

That's some bedside manner, Val thought wryly, watching the little scene, and wondered once again what he was doing here. He *was* a doctor, after all. Perhaps he'd been called in on a consultation. But what did a research cardiologist know about broken bones? It was hardly his area of expertise.

With a brief nod in her direction, he turned on his heel and walked out of the room.

'Sit down, Val,' Myra said when he was gone. 'What lovely flowers! So cheerful. Thanks very much.'

Val set the vase of flowers down on the dresser across the room, then came back and sat in the chair next to the bed. She was dying to ask Myra about Michael, but before she could make up her mind to actually do it Myra herself went on to explain.

'Michael and his mother have both been so good to me since the accident,' she said in a decidedly shaky voice.

Val gave her a sharp look. The girl appeared to be terribly nervous. Her lower lip was quivering, and she was twisting the sheet around tightly in her fingers. It could just be weakness from her injuries, but it seemed to Val that it was something more than that.

'Well, they probably feel David was responsible,' she replied slowly. 'After all, he was driving.'

'Yes, but what they don't know——' She broke off, biting her lip and reddening, and Val could see the sparkle of tears in her eyes.

'What is it, Myra?' she asked softly. 'Are you in pain? Shall I call for a nurse?'

Myra turned her head to face her, the tears still glinting in her eyes. 'Oh, Val, I'm so glad you came. You're the only one I can talk to, the only one who might understand.'

'Yes?' Val prompted. 'Understand what?'

'About David and me.'

Val's eyes widened in surprise. 'You and David?' she echoed.

Myra nodded. 'We'd been seeing each other for some time. In fact we'd even discussed getting married.'

'Oh, Myra,' Val said, touched. 'I'm so sorry.'

Myra heaved a deep sigh. 'I don't know whether you realised it or not, but even all those years ago when we were kids in school I was crazy about him.' She smiled sadly. 'And all he could think of was you. When you left town, I was glad. I thought I'd have a chance at him at last.'

Val stared at her, stunned, at a total loss for words. It had never crossed her mind that Myra had been interested in David.

Finally she managed to stammer out, 'I had no idea.'

'But it didn't work out that way,' Myra went on. 'After you left, he just seemed to go further and further downhill. Oh, he'd call me when he was lonely, but you were always the one he really wanted. Then, about a year ago, he suddenly seemed to be getting his act together. I was so happy. I thought it might have been because of me, that I'd really helped him in some way, just by being there for him, loving him so much.'

'Well, I'm glad,' Val said helplessly. 'And I'm sure you did help him.'

Myra lay her head back and stared blankly up at the ceiling. 'Then you came back,' she went on in a flat, toneless voice. 'I even agreed with him that it would be a good thing if you and he could see each other again, to make sure you really were out of his system for good.' She turned to look at Val, blinking away the tears. 'I could have kicked myself when I saw you together that night at the reunion party. So to get him away from you I encouraged him to have a drink. One drink led to another. We went off in the car, and you know what happened then.'

'But didn't you realise?' Val asked, leaning closer and gazing down earnestly at the girl. 'Didn't he tell you? We *did* have a good talk that night, and David agreed with me that it was all over between us, that it had been for years. It was only puppy love, habit. In fact, when I saw him dancing with you, it seemed obvious that you were the one he really cared about, not me.'

Myra raised herself up on one elbow and gave Val a stricken look. 'Yes, I do know that. He told me later in the car.' She flopped her head back on the pillow. 'But by then it was too late. He was already drunk, out of control.'

The tears began to flow in earnest then. Val got up from the chair. This kind of emotional upset couldn't possibly be doing Myra any good. But before she left, she had to ask one more question.

'Myra,' she asked softly, 'have you told any of this to David's mother? Or his brother?'

'Oh, no!' Myra gulped. She clutched at Val's hand. 'And you've got to promise me you won't tell them, either. I couldn't bear it, living in the same town with his mother and having her know what I did.'

'All right,' Val said. 'I won't. I promise. But you know, Myra, it wasn't your fault what happened to David. He's the one who decided to take the drink.' She gently removed her hand. 'I think I should leave now. You need to rest.'

'Will you come back to see me again?'

Val hesitated. 'I'm not sure yet what my plans are,' she said slowly. 'But if I do decide to stay a while longer in Carleton, yes, of course I'll come to see you again.'

She replaced the screen around the bed and walked softly over to the door. Her head was whirling, her thoughts in a turmoil. What a terrible thing for poor Myra to have to live with. If only she could convince her to tell the truth about what had really happened that night, she herself would be entirely exonerated in the eyes of David's family.

She paused at the door, half inclined to go back and plead with Myra to do just that. But in the end she decided that nothing would really be gained. David's mother had already assured her she didn't in any way blame her. Even Michael seemed to be far less hostile towards her now.

It really made no difference at this point. In any case, she'd be going home soon and would most likely never see any of these people again. They'd have to work out their little drama by themselves. Her role in it was over.

When she stepped out into the corridor, however, she almost bumped into Michael Prescott himself. He was standing just outside the door with his back to her, his hands in his pockets. She stopped short. She'd thought he'd already left. Apparently he'd been waiting for her to go so he could go back and finish his visit with Myra.

When he turned around to face her, she nodded at him and gave him a tight little smile, then started to walk past him. But before she'd gone two steps, he reached out a hand to stop her.

'I was waiting for you,' he said.

Startled, Val looked over at him. 'For me?' she asked.

He took her lightly by the elbow and began guiding her down the long corridor. Totally bewildered, she automatically followed along.

'I thought if you had no other plans you might have lunch with me,' he said as they went.

When they came to the lift, he dropped his hand and put it back in his trouser pocket. She looked up at him, really seeing him for the first time that day. He was dressed casually in dark trousers and a pale grey jersey shirt that dimmed the blue of his eyes into an even more glacial hue.

Still, he was smiling at her pleasantly enough. And in seeking her out last night just in order to apologise, he'd made a friendly enough gesture. Why not have lunch with him? She didn't have another blessed thing to do that afternoon.

'All right,' she said.

They stepped into the waiting lift, which was full of people, and when they reached the main floor they made their way towards the entrance. He held the door open for her, and they walked outside into the bright sunshine.

'Is there any place special you'd like to go?' he asked.

She was about to say she didn't care, but then she remembered that just the day before Jack Thompson had taken his children to one of her favourite old haunts. It was such a beautiful day. Why not?

'I wonder if the little café at Marsh Creek is still there?' she asked him.

'Let's find out,' he replied promptly.

They had reached his car, a silvery grey Jaguar. He opened the door for her, then came around and got in the driver's seat. It was stifling inside the car, and he quickly started the engine.

'The air-conditioning will take a few minutes to get going,' he said. He put the car in gear and deftly backed out of the parking slot. 'Do you swim?' he asked.

She nodded. 'Yes, although I don't get much chance in Seattle, at least not outdoors. The weather, you know.'

'It's a good day for it. We can probably rent suits out there if you'd like.'

As they drove the five miles out of town to the small resort, Val gazed out of the window at the passing scenery, amazed at how little things had changed in ten years. Every landmark was still there, still recognisable. The dry rolling hills, the houses along the way, the trees—pepper, oak, fig, apricot—even the same bright orange California poppies bloomed in the ditches at the side of the road.

The intervening years simply melted away. It was as though she'd never been gone. She felt like the same carefree schoolgirl she'd been then, and it suddenly struck her that her heart was lighter, her spirits higher, than at any time since.

It was also pleasant to be driven along in the sleek car, quite cool now that the air-conditioning was functioning, and by such an attractive man. She gave him a quick glance out of the corner of her eye. He was lounging back casually in his seat, his large hands resting on the steering-wheel, and in profile he looked even more devastating.

The short-sleeved grey shirt revealed strong forearms, lightly covered with black hair, not heavily muscled, but taut and firm. The only jewellery he wore was a thin gold watch with a wide leather band. Val had a slightly giddy sensation, as though she was on the brink of an exciting adventure of some kind, and couldn't quite suppress a small smile of satisfaction.

'What's funny?' Michael said in an amused tone.

'Funny?' Val asked. Then she realised he'd noticed the smile. 'Oh, nothing. I was just feeling rather carefree.'

He gave her a quick glance. 'Is that so unusual?'

She laughed. 'Well, I guess so. This is the first real vacation I've had in some time.'

'Sounds as if your life might be rather grim.'

'No, not grim,' she said thoughtfully. 'But I work hard, and I take my job seriously.'

'What is your job?'

'I'm a buyer for a rather nice boutique in Seattle.'

'Do you like the work?'

'Oh, yes. I love it.'

'Well, that's the important thing.'

They had reached their turn-off now, and Michael guided the car into the narrow rutted road towards the entrance. It was all exactly as Val remembered it. The small wooden sign at the gate, with the letters 'Marsh Creek' burned into it, the pavilion over to one side where they used to dance. Even now she could hear the music from the jukebox, different from the tunes that had been popular then, but with the same kind of rhythm.

Michael pulled up at the gate and wound the window down to pay the entrance fee to the waiting attendant. The pungent smell of chlorine from the pool drifted inside through the open window, and the music, the shouts of the crowd, were much louder.

He parked under the shade of a gigantic old fig tree, still sparsely hung with black fruit, the hornets buzzing around the rotting figs that had fallen on the ground.

'Which would you rather do first?' Michael asked as they got out of the car. 'Swim or eat?'

Val glanced at her watch. It was past twelve. 'I'm rather hungry at the moment,' she said.

'All right. Lunch first, then maybe a swim afterwards.'

The small restaurant was still there, just beyond the dance pavilion and overlooking the outdoor pool. They made their way through the crowd of young people gyrating on the dance-floor to the pounding beat of a rock band coming over the loudspeaker system, and went through the heavy glass doors.

It was relatively quiet inside the restaurant, which was almost empty. It didn't look terribly clean, either. There were napkins and cigarette butts strewn on the dusty floor, and most of the tables were still littered with dirty dishes.

'It doesn't look very popular,' Michael murmured at her side as they walked over to a clean table by the window. 'I wonder if there's some kind of message to that.'

Val turned and gave him a quick smile. 'I don't think that's necessarily a commentary on the food. Most people who come out here bring their own picnic lunches.'

'I hope you're right,' he said with feeling.

'Although,' she added, wrinkling her nose, 'I don't recall it being quite this messy.'

They sat down and consulted the fly-specked menus, which offered the same choices Val remembered from the old days—hamburgers, hot dogs, grilled cheese sandwiches, and, of course, soft drinks.

After one cursory glance, Michael set his menu down and gave her a wry questioning look. 'Are you sure you want to eat here?'

Val laughed. 'It doesn't look too appetising, does it? The only thing that's changed in ten years is the prices.'

'Well, if you're game, I guess I am, too,' he said dubiously.

A bored young man in a grimy apron came over and set down glasses of water on the table, then stood waiting for their order, his stubby pencil poised over his pad.

'What'll it be?' he drawled lazily.

Val looked up at him. 'I'll have a jumbo cheese-burger, everything on it, and a small Coke.'

Michael nodded. 'Make mine the same.' When the boy had gone, he leaned back in his chair and eyed her quizzically. 'I only hope we don't end up with food poisoning. Remember, it was your choice.'

'Chalk it up to nostalgia,' she said lightly. 'Recap-turing my misspent youth.'

'You're hardly old enough for that,' he said.

He raised his glass of water and held it up to the light, examining it suspiciously. Then he shrugged, put it to his mouth and drained it.

Val watched, mesmerised by every movement he made. He was so intensely *male*! Even so, she was still wary of the man, even slightly suspicious of the abrupt change in his attitude towards her. For some reason, in spite of his physical appeal, she felt she had to be on her guard against his good looks, his easy charm.

She turned and gazed out of the window, frowning slightly. It was probably just her old paranoia. A psychiatrist could no doubt trace her indifference to men, which verged on a phobia, to her wayward father. But she wasn't in the least indifferent to Michael Prescott, and that was what worried her.

'Is something wrong?' he asked quietly.

She turned back to him, amazed at how he picked up on her moods so accurately. It was a new experience for her. Most of the men she knew were primarily interested in two things—their own careers and getting her into bed with as little preliminary as possible.

She'd learned how to avoid the latter, adroitly, and without too many hurt feelings or wounded egos, but she was genuinely fascinated by anyone's career and never had to pretend an interest she didn't feel.

He was still watching her, waiting for an answer.

'No,' she said. 'Nothing's wrong. I was only daydreaming.' She took a sip of water, then smiled at him. 'Tell me about your work, Michael.'

'Well, you probably already know I'm a doctor. I specialise in cardiology.'

'That sounds like very satisfying work. Are you one of those surgeons who do heart transplants?'

'God, no!' he said brusquely. 'I'm mostly involved in research.'

He went on to tell her about the foundation in Los Angeles that funded his project, which was aimed primarily at diminishing the risk of heart disease through exercise and diet. When their lunch arrived, he pointed down at the enormous cheeseburger set before him with a rueful smile.

'This is a perfect example of what we shouldn't eat,' he commented drily.

He then proceeded to devour it with gusto, and Val joined him. In spite of the tacky atmosphere and suspect cleanliness of the little café, the food tasted wonderful to her, just as good as she remembered it.

'Ah,' she said when she had finished, 'I haven't had a cheeseburger that good in years.'

He grinned at her. 'Part of it is still on your mouth.' He reached across the table and dabbed lightly at her lips with his napkin. 'There, that's better.'

Val was touched by the intimate gesture, and more than a little puzzled. Just yesterday this man had stood looming over her at his mother's house treating her like dirt under his feet. Now today he was a different person, courteous, kind, even tender, and acting as though he really liked her.

He leaned back in his chair and lit a cigarette, then raised it in the air and shook his head. 'This is another thing we warn people against. However,' he added, 'I believe in moderation in all things, and there are times when tobacco really hits the spot.' He held out the packet to her. 'I'm sorry. Do you want one?'

'No, thanks. That isn't one of my vices.'

He raised an eyebrow and replaced the packet in his shirt pocket. 'What are your vices, then?'

His voice was low, even suggestive, and Val's guard came up immediately. 'I'm afraid you wouldn't find them interesting,' she murmured dismissively.

Once again, he seemed to be tuned into her every changing mood, and abruptly changed the subject. 'So, you live in Seattle,' he commented in a chatty tone.

She looked over at him in some surprise. 'Yes. Didn't you know that?'

'Actually, I know very little about you at all, except——' He broke off and waved a hand dismissively in the air. 'But that's in the past. Now I'd like to learn more about you.'

Val gave him a direct look. 'Why?' she asked carefully.

He slowly and methodically stubbed out his cigarette in the little metal ashtray on the table, then returned her gaze unflinchingly. 'Why does anyone want to know about another person?' he asked. 'Don't you find other people's lives interesting?'

'Well, yes,' she replied. 'Of course I do.'

'Actually,' he went on. 'I do have rather a more personal interest in anyone who lives in Seattle.'

'Why is that?'

'I've recently been offered a position there, as head of a new research project at the university hospital.'

'I see,' she replied slowly.

Her heart picked up a beat. Perhaps this short encounter wouldn't be the end of their relationship after all. Somehow that shed an entirely new light on it, changed everything.

'Are you going to accept it?' she asked.

'I haven't decided. I like what I'm doing well enough right where I am. What I don't like, however, is living in the Los Angeles area. The smog is killing, and it's terribly crowded. More people seem to flock there every year.'

'Well, Seattle has its share of smog, I'm afraid,' she said. 'And it's growing, too. Have you ever been there?'

'Oh, yes. Several times. There are problems similar to any large metropolitan area, but it certainly has to be one of the most beautiful cities in the world. It also has unique recreational opportunities. What other city can offer boating, fishing, mountain climbing and skiing all within only an hour's drive apart?'

She laughed. 'You sound like a representative of the Chamber of Commerce.' She hesitated, then added lightly, 'It also sounds as though you've already made up your mind to take the job.'

He shook his head slowly and gave her a crooked smile. 'No, I haven't. Not yet. There are several other factors to consider.'

For some reason, the way he smiled, the tone of his voice, his whole manner, made Val feel as though she herself might be one of those factors. But that was crazy! They'd really only just met.

The waiter came over with their bill just then. Michael glanced at it, then reached in his hip pocket for his wallet. After paying the bill, he rose from his chair and stood looking down at her.

'How about a walk to work off some of the cheeseburger?' he suggested. 'Then we can have a swim.'

They left the pavilion and began to stroll leisurely along the paths through the wooded area surrounding the pool, threading their way among the picnicking families and clusters of young people for close to an hour. On a wide stretch of grass a volleyball game was in progress, and the laughter of the players, the loud music from the Walkmans, the shrieks of children filled the air.

Each sight brought back a flood of pleasant memories to Val from her own girlhood—as a child, coming out here with her parents and their friends before her father's drinking problem had spoiled every aspect of family life, then later, with her own crowd from school almost every weekend during the summer.

Michael was an ideal companion, casual and relaxed, silent for the most part, but occasionally pointing out a small homely drama to her with genuine amusement—a mother consoling a bawling child, lovers entwined on a blanket under the shade of a tree, a little boy trying to master walking on a pair of stilts who kept falling off and getting right back up again.

It gave her a heady feeling, too, to meander slowly around the familiar territory with such a tall, good-looking man at her side. For the most part he treated her in a friendly, but rather distant fashion, and, except for one incident, when she almost tripped over a stone in her path and he gripped her firmly by the arm to keep her from falling, he didn't touch her once.

Back at the pool, they rented bathing suits, towels and a blanket from the attendant, and while Val's one-piece model wasn't exactly the height of fashion it fitted her well and blessedly wasn't too revealing. Although she had a slim figure, with good legs, a narrow waist and high, firm breasts, she was still a little shy about appearing half-naked in front of Michael.

When they met again outside the dressing-rooms, she was all prepared for a quick once-over from those penetrating blue eyes, but what she wasn't prepared for was the sight of Michael himself in his dark cotton trunks.

His chest was much broader and his shoulders much wider than they had appeared with clothes on. His bathing suit was of a heavy material, as modestly cut as her own, but it did hang rather low on his lean hips, revealing a light sprinkling of coarse black hair that tapered down from his chest and over his stomach into a thin line that disappeared inside the waistband.

When she realised that he was gazing rather fixedly at her as well, she reddened slightly and clutched her towel to her chest.

He held out a hand. 'Well, are you all ready to take the plunge?'

Her heart turned over. She knew quite well that he was referring to diving into the pool, but somehow his words struck her as having a deeper significance than that, and as she took his outstretched hand even that slight contact was unsettling to her, an odd mixture of pleasure and trepidation.

'I'm game if you are,' she replied lightly.

They went over to the pool, and side by side dived into the deep end. When Val came up for air, panting from the shock of the unexpectedly cool water, he was treading water just a few feet away from her, shaking his head, the drops on his broad, tanned shoulders sparkling in the bright sunshine.

She had pinned her hair back loosely, but in the impact of the dive it had come undone, and was now streaming wetly over her forehead and into her eyes. Laughing, Michael reached out a hand to smooth it back.

'You look as if you're about ten years old,' he said. Then his gaze dropped to her still heaving breast, and he grinned crookedly. 'Well, not quite,' he amended wickedly.

Flustered at the frank commentary, she ducked her head under water and swam away from him. The pool was so crowded and he was such a strong swimmer, however, that she didn't get far. When he caught up with her, she had just come up again for air.

'Let's see if we can get in a lap or two through all these bodies,' he shouted above the noise. 'That's about all I can take of this.'

She nodded, and they swam together in whatever open spaces they could find for two lengths. When she reached the edge of the pool, he was already standing on the concrete apron, a hand held out to help her up.

They spread their blanket down on a fairly private open stretch of grass under the shade of an enormous old live oak tree, some distance away from the pool. Michael immediately flopped down on his back and closed his eyes, while Val sat a few feet away from him, drying off and running her fingers through her wet hair to straighten out the tangles.

After a few moments, he seemed to have fallen asleep, and she could watch him unobserved. He was leaning back against the trunk of the tree, his long legs outstretched, his arms folded over his chest, and he looked the picture of relaxed contentment.

After their shaky beginning yesterday, she'd enjoyed the outing with him more than she would have dreamed possible. He was fun to be with, considerate, attractive; in fact, she found almost everything about him very appealing.

It was an important 'almost'. She still couldn't quite fight down a nagging sense of doubt, a tiny pinprick of anxiety that it couldn't possibly be this easy. There had to be a catch somewhere, but at the moment she couldn't put her finger on what it might be. He was almost *too* attractive, *too* nice. In her experience men like that were practically an extinct species. And always married to someone else.

Then, suddenly, she saw a lazy smile curve on his lips, his eyes flashed open, and she found herself staring directly into them, so brilliant that they dazzled her. She flushed with embarrassment. He hadn't been asleep after all. It was too late to look away. She could only sit there, mesmerised by the steady blue glare.

CHAPTER FOUR

STILL holding Val's gaze in his, Michael raised himself up on one elbow and shifted his body the few feet that separated them. He reached out a hand and touched her hair, which had dried by now.

'I like your hair hanging loose like that,' he murmured lazily. 'You should always wear it that way.'

He was so close to her that she could smell the chlorine on his skin, see the light sheen of perspiration on his forehead, the dark stubble of beard on his chin. For a moment, she was so strongly tempted to bend her head down and meet his lips with her own that she was afraid she'd actually do it.

Quickly, she turned from him and scanned the surrounding area. It was just a little after three o'clock, and, although the summer sun was still high in the sky, it was screened by the tall poplars that rose up on the western edge of the picnic grounds. By now it was almost deserted.

'How long do you plan to stay in Carleton?' she heard Michael ask her.

She turned back to him. 'At the moment, that's debatable. Although I came down especially for the reunion party, I had planned to spend two weeks after that visiting with an old friend of mine, Bonnie Thompson. But now...' She shrugged, shying away from the painful subject of David's death. 'Now I don't know. The Thompsons have an epidemic of measles on their hands and are pretty well housebound, so there doesn't seem much point in my hanging around.'

'I'd like to have you stay,' he said in a low voice.

Her eyes widened in surprise. 'But your mother said you yourself were leaving in a few days.'

'I had planned to, yes. But I could be talked into extending my visit.' He smiled. 'With the proper incentive.'

He wanted her to stay! Did she want to? With all her heart, she thought fervently. But was it such a good idea? Where could it possibly lead? All her old suspicions came bubbling to the surface, warning her to tread carefully.

She hardly knew the man, but there was one thing certain—he was already beginning to wield tremendous power over her. She would be no match for him in any game he cared to play, and, although she was strongly tempted simply to follow along wherever he led her, the prospect also seemed vaguely threatening.

Then he frowned. 'Perhaps I was premature in asking you to stay on in Carleton.'

'What do you mean?' she asked guardedly.

'Well, for all I know, you could already be involved in an important relationship. Even engaged.' He glanced down at her hand, lying on top of the blanket. 'Although I haven't noticed a ring. Or is that an old-fashioned notion?'

'No,' she said shortly. 'I'm not involved with anyone. How about you?'

He shook his head firmly. 'No. There's no one.'

'I thought all busy doctors needed long-suffering wives to keep the home fires burning for them,' she commented lightly.

He laughed shortly. 'I tried that once, and, believe me, it doesn't work out that way.'

'You've been married, then?'

He made a dismissive gesture with his hand. 'If you could call it a marriage. It was while I was in medical school, many long years ago. Sixteen, to be exact. I was barely twenty-two, she was only nineteen and wanted to be married to a doctor a hell of a lot more than she wanted to be married to me.' He laughed harshly. 'She soon found out that there was very little similarity between a penurious, hard-working medical student and the affluent doctors she'd seen on television.'

'I'm sorry,' Val said softly.

He shrugged. 'Oh, don't be. That's ancient history. It only lasted a year, and then we went our separate ways, with the utmost relief on both sides, I might add.' He grinned. 'I heard later that she married her gynaecologist. Twenty years her senior and already rich.'

'Well, at least there weren't any children to worry about. I always think they're the ones to suffer most from divorce.'

'No,' he replied slowly. 'There were no children. Thank God!' he added with feeling.

'Do you have something against children?' she asked with a smile.

'No. Not if there's a stable home environment to raise them in. Like you, I believe it's necessary to build a solid marriage first before bringing children into the world.' He smiled wryly. 'I haven't noticed very many of those around.'

Val thought about her own family life. After her father started drinking, all she could remember were arguments and a constant atmosphere of tension. Although her parents were never divorced, they might as well have been, probably should have been.

Suddenly, he raised himself up to a sitting position. He leaned closer towards her so that the bare skin of his chest just grazed her shoulder, and reached out a hand to touch her lightly on her arm. She drew in a sharp breath and held it in as he bent his head to brush his lips lightly, tentatively over her forehead.

When she made no move to draw away, the hand on her arm tightened. She turned her body slightly towards him and stared directly into his eyes, searching for some clue as to what he was thinking and feeling.

His expression was quite serious, but the blue eyes glowed brightly. Was it desire, she wondered, or only the dancing shafts of sunlight that streamed intermittently through the tall trees?

All she could do was sit there, waiting, unable to move a muscle. She knew he was going to kiss her, and, although she wanted it, even ached to feel his mouth on hers, his arms around her, his body pressed close to hers, at the same time she feared it.

He cupped her face in his hands and gazed into her eyes for a moment. Then he smiled, his dark head dipped down again, and she felt the first gentle pressure of his mouth on hers. His lips were soft and dry, and, while there was nothing threatening about his kiss, the way his mouth moved on hers was so subtly seductive that she found her own lips parting slightly in an instinctive, unthinking response.

Then, at the same time, she felt the tip of his tongue seeking entry to her mouth and one hand sliding down from her shoulder to brush lightly over her breast.

Alarmed, she broke off the probing kiss abruptly and drew her head back. The hand on her breast stilled, then returned to her shoulder. She stared at him wide-eyed. Although the light of desire still glittered in his eyes, he seemed to be in perfect control of himself.

He gave her a crooked smile. 'I think perhaps we'd better go,' he said lightly. 'How about it?' He drew away from her and rose to his feet.

'Yes, of course,' she replied. She got up to stand beside him. 'I suppose it is about time we got back.'

The moment had passed, and as they walked slowly back to the dressing-rooms Val had the sinking feeling that it would never come again.

By the time she'd changed back into her street clothes, she was plunged into a glum reverie of regret. What had made her draw away from him that way? She had enjoyed his kiss, had waited for it expectantly all afternoon, in fact, had wanted it from the moment she'd seen him standing in the hospital corridor outside Myra's room that morning waiting for her.

She'd ruined everything now with her same old crippling fear of intimacy. Here was the first man to come along since David who really set her pulses racing, and she'd managed to discourage him before he'd done one thing to offend her.

They drove back in almost total silence to the hospital where Val had left her car, each apparently deep in thought. Although Val felt decidedly let down by the abrupt ending to an almost perfect day, it was no more than she'd expected.

When they reached the hospital car park, she pointed out her rental car to him, and he pulled up alongside it. She opened her door quickly, so that he wouldn't have to get out, then turned to him with a polite smile.

'Thanks a lot, Michael,' she said, 'for a lovely afternoon. I enjoyed it very much.' She grinned. 'Especially the wonderful cheeseburger.'

He dipped his dark head. 'My pleasure. I enjoyed it, too. I'm sorry to cut it short, but I have some business to take care of for my mother before five o'clock.'

She nodded. 'Yes, of course. Well . . .' She started to get out of the car.

'If you have no other plans,' he added quickly, 'perhaps we could have dinner together this evening. We could even drive into San Francisco if we got an early start.'

Val's heart turned over. 'Yes,' she replied slowly. 'I'd like that.'

'It will take at least an hour to get into the city,' he went on. 'Let's say I pick you up at the hotel around six-thirty. Or is that calling it too close?'

'No, that sounds fine.'

'Good. I'll see you then.'

She stepped out on to the hot pavement, but before she could close the door behind her he had called her name. She turned back and leaned down to peer inside the car. He was looking at her with a strange, almost diffident expression on his face.

'Yes?' she said.

'Would you mind very much leaving your hair that way?'

She raised a hand to run it over her shaggy sun-dried mop. 'You can't be serious!' she exclaimed, laughing. 'It's a mess!'

'But I like it,' he announced firmly.

'Well, I'll see what I can do.'

It had been a long time since Val had dressed to go out on a date with such a feeling of excited anticipation—so long, in fact, that she couldn't even remember when it had been.

As she showered and washed her hair, she hummed a little tune under her breath, and even occasionally broke out into loud song, albeit slightly off-key. She felt just like a romantic schoolgirl, and even though she warned herself over and over again not to get her hopes up or count on anything she simply couldn't quite suppress the compelling images and romantic fantasies, all starring Michael Prescott, that kept rising up in her mind.

He would be so easy to fall in love with, she thought, as she stepped out of the shower and dried off. How he had managed to remain unattached for so long was beyond her. Of course there was no future in the relationship. She knew that. They'd both be leaving Carleton soon. She would probably never see him again.

There was, however, the job he'd mentioned in Seattle. If he were to decide to take that, who knew where it would lead? And he had asked her to extend her stay in Carleton for his sake. There wasn't a reason in the world why she shouldn't. Even if nothing ever came of it, why not enjoy the time they did have together? At least she'd have a pleasant memory to look back on.

Still, something didn't ring quite true about the whole affair, and now that he was gone that factor loomed even larger. Away from his disturbing presençe, the magnetism of his sheer physical appeal, her doubts only escalated.

It just wasn't logical. Why would a man who had made no secret of his loathing for her one day suddenly turn around the next and pursue her as though she were the girl of his dreams?

Val had no false modesty about her looks. Not only did she have a naturally good bone-structure and pleasant, even features, but she took great pains with her appearance. She had to in her job. But even though sometimes it seemed as though she spent her whole social life doing nothing but fending off unwelcome advances from predatory males, she knew quite well she was no great beauty, no seductive siren.

Michael didn't *act* like a predator. He hadn't pushed when she'd broken away from him. However, rather than feeling reassured by his restraint, she only found it alarming, even a little calculating.

Right now, it was time to get ready, and since this could be the only night they'd ever have together she wanted to make a memorable impression. She padded barefoot over to the wardrobe in her terry-cloth robe, a towel wrapped loosely around her damp head, to survey the possibilities hanging there.

She was glad now that she'd collected such an extensive wardrobe through her work. Thinking she'd be away from home for almost three weeks, she'd also brought along a wide variety of summer outfits. Nothing too provocative, but decidedly feminine. And since they were going into the city, it should be something dressy.

She finally decided on a pale yellow silk peau-de-soie, the bodice cut quite low and held up by thin straps, the skirt tucked with tiny pleats at the waist, then tapering down to a narrower hemline. She'd carry the matching stole for warmth in case it grew cool later on, but also for modesty's sake. She'd never worn the dress before, and had bought it on a wild impulse when it had come in the boutique, just because it fitted her so well and the colour was so good with her blonde-streaked hair.

She sat down at the dressing-table to tackle her shoulder-length hair. He had asked her to leave it loose, and she intended to do so if it killed her. Ordinarily, she wore it tucked back behind her ears in a loose bun, but it did have enough natural wave so that when she brushed it vigorously it framed her face rather nicely.

Make-up wasn't difficult. Since she had a naturally good colour and tanned evenly, very little was necessary, just a light sprinkling of powder, a dash of coral lip-gloss and a careful, subdued application of eye-liner and mascara.

A few thin gold chains around her neck, a pair of looped gold earrings, the strappy high-heeled sandals that just matched the dress, and she was ready. She picked up her bag and glanced at her watch. It was twenty-five minutes past six. Time to leave.

She took one last look at herself in the mirror, and her heart sank. The reflection of a stranger was gazing back at her. The dress was too suggestive, the hair-style too wanton, the jewellery too garish. She looked like a siren on the prowl, just asking for a night of seduction.

What could she do? It was too late to change. No, it wasn't. Yes, it was. She stood for a full five minutes in an agony of indecision, and finally realised she had to do *something*!

She ran to the wardrobe. Maybe the dress she'd worn to the reunion dinner. But that had to go over her head, and she'd need to redo her hair and make-up.

'Now, stop it!' she cried aloud, stamping her foot.

She was acting just like a schoolgirl on her first date. She glanced in the mirror again, trying to make an objective assessment. There was nothing cheap about her appearance. She looked like a woman who had dressed to please a man. What was wrong with that? She just wasn't used to it.

In the end, however, just to be on the safe side, she arranged the stole so that it loosely covered her bare shoulders, and looped it in front of the low bodice. That would have to do. It was already a quarter to seven.

She took a deep breath and went down to the lobby to meet him.

He was waiting for her by the front desk, leaning back against it as though he owned the hotel, lazily surveying the people passing by out of half-closed eyes.

He looked absolutely devastating, the reality far surpassing the mental images, and as Val came out of the lift she stood there for a few seconds watching him, drinking her fill of the tall, elegant picture he made.

He was dressed rather formally in a beautifully tailored dark suit, crisp white shirt and striped tie. At that moment, he could have carried her off to the ends of the earth, and she would have jumped at the chance.

She started to walk towards him. As though sensing her presence, he straightened up and his head came around, watching her approach. His gaze was frankly appraising, but not brazenly so, and when she reached him the light in his eyes was unmistakable.

'I'm sorry I'm late,' she apologised. 'Usually I'm very prompt.'

'That's all right,' he said, his glance flicking over her. 'It was worth the wait.' He gave her a warm smile and reached out a hand to touch her loosely waving hair. 'Shall we go?'

Since Carleton was almost fifty miles north-east of San Francisco and just a little too far for commuters to travel, it had remained relatively unspoiled through the years of tremendous growth in the whole Bay Area. The one industry in town, a sugar refinery, still sustained the small local population, which hadn't varied by so much as a hundred souls one way or the other in living memory.

It was a lovely balmy evening, the midsummer sun still hanging low in the western sky, suffusing the dry rolling hills with a golden glow. As they drove along the two-lane country roads that led to the interstate into the city, they chatted mainly about Michael's work, which Val found truly fascinating. She kept hoping he would bring up the subject of the position he'd been offered in Seattle, but he didn't refer to it once.

By the time they reached the Oakland side of the bridge that spanned San Francisco Bay, the sun had set and dusk was beginning to fall. In the distance, the lights of the city twinkled brightly in the gathering dark, and as they approached the high, graceful bridge Val felt once again the same sensation of excited anticipation she remembered from the old days.

Only tonight, that feeling was enhanced a hundredfold by the presence of the man sitting beside her. The traffic had thickened considerably, and since he had to concentrate all his attention on manoeuvring his way through it they drove the rest of the way in silence. He was a careful driver, but not an overly cautious one, and once on the San Francisco side of the bay even the horrendous early evening traffic on the steep city streets didn't seem to ruffle his calm, authoritative composure.

He had chosen one of San Francisco's most elegant restaurants, perched high on a rocky slope overlooking Seal Beach and the Golden Gate. When they stepped into the ornate foyer, it was obvious that he was well known to the *maître d'hotel*, who greeted them effusively at the entrance.

'Good evening, Dr Prescott,' he said, bowing and scraping before them. 'It's nice to have you back with us again.'

He led them to a secluded table by the long window wall, where they could look out at the crashing phosphorescent surf far below and the lights of the bridge outlined against the dark blue sky to the north.

'That's not like any *maître d'* I've ever come across,' Val said in a low voice when they were seated alone at their table.

Michael laughed. 'All that attention wasn't because of my *beaux yeux*,' he said. 'I hate to admit it, but I've greased many a palm here in the past several years.'

'How do you manage that?' she asked lightly. 'I mean, I thought you lived in Los Angeles.'

'That's hardly the end of the earth. I make a point of coming up to the Bay Area about once a month.'

It was on the tip of her tongue to ask him if those trips were private social jaunts, perhaps with female companionship, or for the purpose of checking in with his mother and brother. However, while she hesitated, the wine steward appeared at the table and stood there expectantly, waiting for their order.

Val looked down to consult the drinks list. The interruption had probably just come in time. It was really none of her business whom he came here with, and the subject of David must still be a sore one with him. She didn't want anything to spoil this lovely evening. For all she knew, it could be the last one they'd ever have.

They both ordered martinis, and when the wine steward had left Michael leaned back in his chair and eyed her appreciatively.

'You know, your hair looks so lovely hanging loose. I can't help wondering why you don't wear it like that all the time.'

'Well, maybe I do,' she said with a little laugh. 'You've only known me a few days, after all.'

'Yes. You're right. Although somehow it seems longer than that.' He shrugged. 'And of course you aren't a complete stranger to me. I just have a hard time connecting the little girl I used to see hanging around the house with the woman you've become.'

Val fiddled nervously with her silverware. He was touching on the very subject she'd decided just a few minutes ago to avoid. She eyed him carefully. He seemed relaxed enough.

'Hardly a little girl,' she said at last. 'After all, David and I——'

Their drinks arrived just then, and she broke off. But even before that, at the first mention of his brother's name, Michael's eyes had glazed over, and in the dim light of the flickering candle on top of the table she could see the muscles of his jaw tense.

She took a quick swallow of her martini and looked around the restaurant. It was heavily carpeted in a lush dark red pile, and the walls were papered in an ornate Victorian pattern of red and gold fleurs-de-lis. The tables were set far enough apart for privacy, each one covered in a heavy white damask cloth. From a far corner came the sounds of a tinkling piano.

The whole atmosphere was subdued and elegant. There was no loud raucous talk or shrill shrieks of hilarity, only a low hum of conversation, punctuated with an occasional burst of sedate laughter. All the patrons were extremely well dressed, many of them in formal evening wear.

Michael stirred the olive around in his drink thoughtfully for a few moments, then raised the glass and took a long swallow. He set it down and leaned forward, his elbows on the table.

'I've been wondering about something ever since we first met,' he said in a dead serious tone.

'Really? What's that?'

'How in the world has a woman like you managed to stay free of a serious relationship all these years?'

This was verging on dangerous territory. Val searched her mind to come up with something that didn't involve David and that old ruined relationship.

'How do you know I have?' she asked lightly, stalling for time.

'Have you been married?'

'No.'

'Engaged?'

'No.'

'Lived with a man?'

'Well, no, but that doesn't mean——'

'Then I was right,' he said with satisfaction. 'I knew it.'

She laughed unsteadily. 'Don't tell me your medical practice involves mind-reading.'

'You still haven't answered my question,' he persisted.

'Well, what about you?' she asked playfully. 'Or perhaps you *are* involved with someone.'

'No, I'm not,' he replied slowly. 'But I already told you why, and I did try it once. Besides, I asked you first.'

'Well, my reasons are probably similar to yours. I've been busy with my work, too. Surely you can understand that, even though it's not as lofty a profession as yours?'

'I don't believe you,' he said flatly. 'It's got to be more than that.'

She had no reply to that. He was right, of course, but she couldn't go into the real reasons with him, not now. She wasn't entirely sure of them herself. Besides, she was far more interested in what was happening to her right now and what might lie in the future than she was in the past.

He was watching her expectantly, waiting for an answer. When several seconds had gone by and she still hadn't said anything, he leaned forward and reached out a hand to cover her own.

'Well, whatever it is,' he said in a low, husky voice, 'I'd like to try to make you forget it.'

Her face grew heated and she stared at him, wide-eyed. What could he mean? His bluntness took her completely off guard. He sounded serious, but wasn't he moving awfully fast on such a short acquaintance?

Suddenly he withdrew his hand and straightened up in his chair. 'Now,' he said, 'would you like another drink, or shall we order dinner?'

'Dinner, I think,' she said weakly.

She took up the large ornate menu and held it up in front of her face so he wouldn't see the deep flush she knew was spreading over it.

The menu offerings, in graceful calligraphic script, swam before her eyes. He had taken the initiative quite firmly from the very beginning, and she had no doubt it would end exactly where he wanted it to. A cold chill gripped her. She was terribly attracted to him, and he must know that.

He didn't mention the subject again all through dinner. She had ended by asking him to order for her, and they shared a delicious Châteaubriand with perfectly cooked vegetables on the side. The wine was a delicious vintage California burgundy.

During dinner he asked her more about her own job, and she went into meticulous detail about every aspect of it, relieved to have a neutral subject to discuss. Besides, she really did love her job, and enjoyed talking about it.

It wasn't until they had finished dinner and were drinking cups of coffee laced with brandy that Michael steered the conversation into more personal channels. He had lit one of his rare cigarettes, and was watching the smoke as it curled up into the air.

'Have you thought any more about extending your stay here in Carleton?' he asked casually.

Since she'd thought about nothing else for the last several hours, she shifted uncomfortably in her chair and stared blankly down at her coffee-cup. Finally, she looked up at him.

'Yes,' she replied. 'I have.'

He raised an eyebrow. 'And what have you decided?'

'Nothing, really.' How could she explain to him that she needed some kind of indication from him of his intentions before she continued on in Carleton just for his sake?

'Well, let me put it this way,' he said in an easy, matter-of-fact tone. 'Which is it? Is there some reason why you want to go back to Seattle right away? Or,' he lowered his voice huskily, 'do you really want to stay but feel you shouldn't?'

Once again, he had read her mood accurately, and she didn't know how to reply. She took another quick sip of her drink to cover her confusion.

'What are you afraid of, Val?' he asked softly.

Startled at the blunt question, she widened her eyes at him. 'Nothing,' she replied quickly. 'Why do you ask?'

He shrugged. 'I'm very attracted to you, you must know that,' he went on. 'And, unless I'm badly mistaken, I think you feel it, too. I can't help wondering why you hesitate to explore it a little further.'

'Is it really that simple, Michael?' she asked.

He smiled. 'That's up to you, isn't it?'

Suddenly she knew he was right. It *was* up to her. Surely by now she could trust herself to handle a relationship with a man, even one as enigmatic and challenging as Michael Prescott. And she wanted to stay, badly.

'Well, all right, then,' she said. 'Then I see no reason why I shouldn't stay—at least a few days longer, anyway.'

He nodded with satisfaction and straightened up in his chair. 'Good,' he said.

The waiter came to ask them if they wanted anything more to eat or drink, and Michael raised an enquiring eyebrow at Val.

'No, thank you,' she said promptly. 'It was wonderful, but I've had more than enough.'

Michael asked for the bill. When he'd signed for it, he got up out of his chair and looked down at her.

'How about a walk?' he asked. 'There's a fairly smooth well-lit path that goes along the top of the cliff. We might even see some seals.'

They made their way to the back entrance and went outside. When the heavy glass door closed behind them, shutting out all the restaurant sounds of music and conversation, it was as though they had stepped into another world, a silent world, with only the crashing of the surf on the rocks below to break the utter stillness of the balmy night.

CHAPTER FIVE

THEY started down the rather steep path that led to the edge of the cliff, but after a few steps Val had to stop, unsure of her footing in her high-heeled sandals.

'Is it too cool for you out here?' Michael asked.

'No,' she replied. 'The slope is just a little difficult in these shoes.'

Immediately his arm came around her shoulders and he hugged her closely to his side. It was a perfectly natural gesture, so right for that particular moment that she leaned against his warmth and strength with a feeling of utter security.

'Better?' he asked, smiling down at her.

She nodded, and they continued down the path until they came to the wooden railing at the edge of the cliff. A million stars dotted the dark night sky, and a bright three-quarter moon cast a pale yellow swath over the sea far below.

Val grasped the wooden railing for support, but Michael kept his arm around her, and as they stood there silently gazing out at the panoramic view his hand began to move slowly up and down her bare arm. Val closed her eyes. She felt as though she were falling. A great surge of tingling warmth flooded through her as his hand continued to move in gentle, rhythmic strokes.

This must be heaven, she thought dreamily—the tall, handsome man at her side, the romantic setting, the delicious feelings welling up inside her. This was what other women felt, talked about, dreamed of, and what she had missed for so long.

His hand stilled on her arm. 'Val,' he said in a low voice.

She opened her eyes and looked up at him. His face was so close to hers now that she could see the moon's reflection in his eyes and catch the scent of his light, musky aftershave.

Immediately, as though she'd given him a sign he'd been waiting for, he put his other arm across her waist, tightening his hold on her. Then his head came down, and his mouth covered hers in a gentle kiss. Val relaxed against him, giving herself up to his warm, mobile mouth, and this time, as the pressure of his kiss gradually increased, became more demanding, she fought down the instinct to back off. This was what she wanted.

His hands left her face and slid down over her neck to her shoulders, slipping underneath the loosely tied stole, which fell unheeded to the ground. His hands were warm on her bare skin, and as he pulled her more tightly up against him his mouth opened wider on hers.

The taste of tobacco and the brandy he had drunk gave her such an exquisitely heady sensation of intimacy that her fears were forgotten and she responded to him without reserve, utterly lost in the moment. It was as though this man, his touch, his scent, his taste, were what she'd been waiting for all her life.

She raised her arms around his neck, yielding and pliant, giving herself up to the moment as his lips opened over hers and his tongue darted past them. The hand on her waist began to travel slowly upwards over the silk bodice of her dress until it settled firmly on her breast, moulding the soft fullness beneath the thin material.

He tore his mouth away from hers and gazed down at her. 'I want you, Val,' he breathed.

As she stared up at him, transfixed by the fire that glowed out of the bright blue eyes, his hand slipped inside the opening of her dress, and she felt his warm, sensitive fingers on the bare skin of her breast. Then, abruptly, he withdrew his hand and brushed it over the front of her dress to smooth it out.

He gave her a crooked smile. 'But obviously now isn't the time or the place. Which brings me to something I have to tell you.'

Oh, lord, she thought in a sudden panic. He *is* involved with someone else. Her whole body went icy cold. She stiffened away from him and forced out a smile.

'Something dreadful?' she asked lightly.

'I don't know. You'll have to be the judge of that. I have to leave for Los Angeles tomorrow. An emergency has come up at the foundation, and it's in an area I'm directly responsible for. Since I was actually supposed to return yesterday, I can hardly refuse to go now that they really need me.'

'I see,' she said with a tight smile. 'I'm sorry.'

'This doesn't have to end here.' He put a hand under her chin and tilted her head up to meet his gaze. 'I want you to come with me,' he said soberly.

She could only stare at him. 'Come with you? You mean to Los Angeles?'

He nodded. 'You said you had two more weeks of your vacation. Come with me, Val. Stay with me.'

Val's head spun. It was the last thing she had expected. Did she want to go? Two weeks with Michael sounded like heaven. But then what? When it was over, she'd go back to her job in Seattle and he'd stay in Los Angeles. Unless—her spirits rose—unless he had decided to accept the offer in Seattle.

But how could she ask him that? Wouldn't such a question imply that she was counting on a possible future together? He wanted her, that much was clear. But how did he feel about her? What were his plans for their relationship, if any?

She looked at him. 'I don't see how I can do that, Michael,' she said slowly at last.

'Why not?' was the prompt rejoinder. 'We're attracted to each other. We're both free, with no other attachments. And we're responsible adults, after all, not children.'

Val gathered all her courage. She had to know. She gave him a direct look and said, 'Before I can make a decision, I need to ask you something.'

He nodded. 'All right,' he said with a smile. 'Fire away.'

She took a deep breath. 'Have you come to a decision yet about the offer in Seattle?'

Immediately the smile faded, and his forehead furrowed in a frown. 'No,' he said. 'I haven't. Does it matter?'

Her heart sank. 'No,' she said. 'I guess not.' She raised a hand and ran it over her hair. 'I'm sorry, Michael. I can't do it. I can't go with you.'

He gave her a sharp look and drew some distance away from her. In the moonlight she could see the frown deepening, the intent, probing look on his face.

'What is it, Val?' he asked carefully. 'Are you looking for promises? Guarantees?'

'Not exactly,' she replied with a shrug. 'I know you're not into commitment, and I don't expect anything like that at this point. But I do need some assurance that at the end of two weeks we won't just say goodbye and never see each other again.'

'I didn't say that. I didn't even mean to imply it. Seattle isn't the end of the earth, after all. There's no reason why we couldn't keep seeing each other, if we both wanted it.'

She shook her head. 'No,' she said firmly. 'I just can't operate that way.'

He sighed heavily and gazed off into the distance. A small black cloud had passed in front of the moon, obscuring his face so that she couldn't make out his expression.

'Well,' he said, turning back to her at last with a wry smile. 'I'm sorry, too, Val. It would have been nice.'

He stooped down to retrieve her stole and placed it carefully around her shoulders. Then, slowly and methodically, he looped one end of it over the other in a rough approximation of the way she'd had it tied before.

It was an intensely sensuous gesture, and although he didn't actually touch her once in the process she was almost painfully aware of his large capable hands hovering so close to the low-cut bodice of her dress as he completed the small task.

'We'd probably better leave,' he said politely, coolly. 'I have an early plane to catch in the morning.'

He placed his hand under her elbow and guided her back up towards the restaurant. They followed the outdoor path around to the front car park, found the Jaguar and got inside.

The trip back to Carleton was a largely silent one. They sat a discreet distance away from each other and, except for an occasional comment on a landmark as they passed by, they seemed to be wrapped in their own thoughts.

The traffic had thinned out considerably at this hour, so that they made much better time, and in less than an hour they were back in Carleton and he had pulled up in front of her hotel.

She turned to him to say goodnight, but he was out of the car and had come around to her side before she'd realised that was his intention. When he opened her door, she got out and stood before him on the pavement.

'Thanks very much for the lovely evening, Michael,' she said in a forced bright tone. 'The dinner was wonderful.'

'My pleasure,' he replied with a brief nod. 'I'll walk you in. Even sleepy old Carleton has its share of muggers, from what I hear.'

She docilely allowed him to take her arm and lead her inside. In the lobby, he punched the button for the lift, then put his hands in his pockets and stared up at the ceiling while they waited in strained silence for what seemed like an eternity. When the lift finally arrived, she thanked him stiffly once again and stepped inside.

'Goodnight, Val,' he said. He held the doors open for a moment, hesitating, then reached in the breast pocket of his jacket, took out a small white card and handed it to her. 'If you change your mind, here are a couple of numbers in Los Angeles where you can reach me. If not, who knows? Perhaps we'll meet again one day.'

With one last, quirky smile, he gave her a little salute, stepped back, and the doors closed, shutting him out.

As the lift started up, Val stared blankly down at the card in her hand, then shoved it hastily into her handbag, as though fearful she might be tempted to use it.

By the time she had arrived at her floor and let herself in her room, she was already bitterly regretting her decision not to go with him. His parting words gave her a little hope that she might see him again some time, but he was probably only being polite. A man like Michael Prescott wouldn't waste his time pursuing an iceberg. Why should he?

She untied the stole and threw it down on the bed, then stood rigidly beside it, her eyes squeezed shut, her fists clenched at her sides, fighting back the tears of sheer anger and frustration and self-contempt. What was wrong with her? Would she never get over these crazy, irrational suspicions? Was she condemned to miss every opportunity that came along just because she was so afraid to trust a man? Any man?

She opened her handbag and took out the card he'd given her. If only he'd said one word that meant he cared something about her, she would have gone with him in a flash. She didn't expect a declaration of undying love or a proposal of marriage, just some indication that she was more to him than a two-week interlude.

Instead, he'd accepted her refusal with good grace. He hadn't pressured her in any way or made any false promises, and she had to wonder now how long she would have held out against him if he *had* pushed.

It was too late now, in any event. Slowly, she tore the card into tiny pieces and dropped them into the waste-paper basket. She knew she'd never use it.

She slipped off her sandals and went into the bathroom. Bracing her hands on the washbasin, she stared bleakly into the mirror. Who was it she was so afraid of, she silently asked her reflection, Michael Prescott or herself?

The next morning, knowing he was gone, out of Carleton, out of her life for good, Val still had slight twinges of regret, but she was also relieved and more convinced than ever that she'd made the right decision.

Things had moved way too fast for her. She'd been virtually swept off her feet, and it was probably better in the long run to lose her chance at him now than to continue getting in deeper and deeper until she was really in over her head.

As soon as she finished her usual light breakfast in the hotel coffee shop, she went back to her room and called Bonnie to tell her she'd decided to go home that day. As she dialled, she braced herself for the onslaught of objections she knew would be forthcoming when her friend heard the news.

Bonnie answered the telephone on the first ring with an abrupt, 'Hello.'

Val was taken aback by the sharp tone of impatience in her voice. Then she heard the children crying noisily in the background and smiled to herself.

'Hey, don't bite my head off,' she said lightly. 'I guess I don't need to ask how things are going.'

Bonnie heaved a dramatic sigh. 'There are times,' she pronounced with solemn deliberation, 'when I really envy you your carefree life. And, believe me, this is one of them.'

Val laughed. 'Sounds as though you have your hands full. How much longer will you be housebound?'

'Today's the last day, thank God, and Jack promised me he'd stay with the little darlings tomorrow afternoon so that you and I could do something interesting together. How about a nice long lunch, with martinis before, wine during, and brandy after? We could go to Columbo's.'

Val hesitated. She'd planned to make her plane reservation and start packing as soon as she finished talking to Bonnie. Now it looked as though she'd have to stay at least one more day. There was no way she could get out of it.

'All right,' she said. 'Sounds great to me.'

'Good. I'll pick you up at the hotel around noon.' The squalling in the background had reached deafening proportions by now. 'Gotta go,' Bonnie shouted over the din. 'See you tomorrow.'

One more day, Val thought as she hung up the receiver. She could stand that. But what in the world was she going to do with herself in the meantime?

She ended up driving into San Francisco for a day's exploration of the city's better dress shops and boutiques, on the basis that she might as well get something constructive accomplished as long as she had to hang around another day.

She had lunch at one of the finest restaurants, justifying her expensive choice by the fact that she was working, after all, and could charge it to her expense account. Actually, after making her rounds that afternoon, she came up with several good advertising and display possibilities for her own shop, as well as finding a wonderful new line of sportswear manufactured by a small local designer house.

When she returned to Carleton late that afternoon, she had a quiet dinner by herself in the hotel dining-room and went to bed early, exhausted from the long day of hiking around the hot, crowded city streets. It had been well worth it, however, on two counts. Not only had she gained important information regarding her job, but she'd managed to keep all thoughts of Michael Prescott at bay during the entire excursion.

The next day at lunch, Bonnie launched immediately into a long recitation of grievances about the endless hours she'd spent imprisoned in her own house with her two sick children. Val was content to let her ramble on. It would do Bonnie good to get it all off her chest, and it saved her from being questioned about her own recent activities.

Finally, fortified by her martini, Bonnie seemed to be winding down. There was a short silence as she raised her glass and took a healthy sip, then she sighed and set the glass down.

'Sorry to bend your ear like that, Val. I really do love my kids, and I'm not a bad mother, but you'll never know what a relief it is to get away from them for a day.'

Val gave her an understanding smile. 'No problem,' she said lightly. 'What are friends for? Are you ready to order?'

'Oh, there's no hurry. I want to hear all about what you've been doing. Although,' she added with an archly knowing smile, 'I think I already have a pretty good idea.'

'Mmm,' Val murmured non-committally. 'Are you psychic?'

Bonnie laughed. 'Hardly! Maybe you've forgotten what a small town can be like. I might have been cooped up for the past few days, but I do have a telephone, and you know how efficiently the Carleton grapevine functions.'

Val only smiled and waited for what she was afraid was coming, while Bonnie drained her martini and raised her hand to signal the waitress for another.

'Now,' she said, leaning back in her chair and fixing Val with a direct look. 'Tell me about you and Michael Prescott.'

Val shook her head. 'I don't believe it!' she exclaimed softly. 'I only saw the man twice. There's nothing to tell.'

'Oh, come on, now,' Bonnie drawled. 'This is me, remember? The last time we talked about him, it didn't sound as though you were ready to start dating the guy. Then the next thing I hear, you're eating lunch and swimming together at Marsh Creek, then having dinner in the city that same night.'

Val thought a minute. It couldn't do any harm to tell Bonnie about her short interlude with Michael, especially since the Carleton communications network had already spread the news. She could well imagine the wild rumours that had circulated by now, and she might as well give Bonnie the correct version.

'All right,' she said, 'I'll tell you exactly what happened. First of all, he called me to apologise for the bad time he gave me that day at his mother's house. Then the next morning I ran into him at the hospital when I went to visit Myra. He invited me to lunch. Since you were housebound and I was rather at a loose end, I accepted. That night we had dinner together in San Francisco. He went back to Los Angeles yesterday morning, and that's all there is to it.'

The waitress came to the table just then with Bonnie's fresh martini. When she was gone, Bonnie stared at Val for several moments, then took a long, slow swallow of her drink and leaned forward across the table.

'And that's *all* that happened?' The disbelief in her voice was unmistakable.

'That's the whole story,' Val replied stoutly.

Bonnie slouched back in her chair. 'I don't believe you,' she said flatly. 'From what I hear, there was more involved than a few meals together.'

Val shrugged. 'Well, Bonnie, all I can tell you is the truth. If you don't believe me——'

'Now, wait just a minute,' Bonnie interrupted, holding up a hand. 'Just about the only thing I really know about Michael Prescott is that he's one of the dreamiest hunks I've ever seen. But I do know you. You haven't changed that much since high school, and you know what I think?'

'No,' Val replied tightly, 'I don't. But I'm sure you're going to tell me.'

'Darn right,' Bonnie said stoutly. 'I think you acted true to form and let him get away. I think here was a gorgeous, successful, *unattached* man interested in you, and you froze.'

'Now, listen, Bonnie,' Val said in a warning tone. 'We're old friends, OK? You may think you have me pegged, but you don't know anything about my life since I left Carleton.'

'Oh, no?' was the swift retort. 'Then please correct me if I'm wrong, but my impression was that you haven't had one even halfway important relationship with a man since you left here. You've as much as told me that yourself.'

To her absolute horror, Val felt her face go up in flame and the tears threaten. When she turned her head away, trying to hide them, Bonnie's hand shot across the table to cover hers.

'Oh, God, I'm sorry, Val,' she said. 'Me and my big mouth. I never will learn to keep my nose out of other people's business. Val, look at me. What can I say to make it better?'

Val forced out a smile and turned back to her friend. 'Never mind me. I know you mean well, Bonnie, but sometimes your comments hit a little too close to home.'

'He asked you to go with him, didn't he?' Bonnie asked in a hushed voice.

Val nodded dumbly. It was far too late to lie now.

'And you turned him down.'

'Well, yes, of course I did. What else could I do?'

'Did you like him? I mean, did you hit it off?'

'Oh, yes,' Val said drily. 'He's a real charmer.'

'Well,' Bonnie said with a sigh, 'I guess you know what you're doing. It just seems a shame, that's all.'

Val shook her head vigorously. 'There's no future in it, Bonnie. I just can't operate that way.'

'You mean without guarantees?'

Val flushed. 'No, of course not. I don't expect an undying declaration of love or promises. But I do need a little caring.'

'He was attracted enough to you to ask you to spend more time with him. Isn't that enough?'

'No. Not for me.'

Bonnie opened her mouth to say something, then bit her tongue. 'OK,' she said with a sigh. 'I won't say another word about it.' She picked up the menu. 'Now, I guess we'd better order.'

They consulted the menus in silence then until the waitress came to take their order. It was almost two o'clock by now, and the restaurant had virtually emptied of the noon-hour rush.

Val closed the menu and handed it to the waitress. 'I'll have a steak sandwich, medium rare, and a green salad.'

'Make mine the same,' Bonnie said.

When the waitress left, Bonnie sat staring down at her empty cocktail glass, turning it around and around on the table-top, her face creased in a frown.

Finally, she raised her eyes and gave Val a direct look. 'You know, I never really did understand what happened before. I mean, why you hightailed it out of town so fast after your parents' accident. I thought for sure you'd marry David and live here the rest of your life. I tried to call you after the funeral, but you'd already disappeared.'

Even after ten years, Val still found the subject painful. She was just about to brush off the probing question with a flip, evasive answer, when she realised from the troubled look on her friend's face that she wasn't just prying, but genuinely concerned. Bonnie had been a loyal friend, and she owed her more than flippancy.

'It's hard to explain,' she said at last. 'You must have known about my father, his drinking.' She laughed bitterly. 'The whole town did by then.'

'I knew he'd lost his job at the mill, and rumour had it that it was because of his drinking.'

Val nodded. 'Well, that was only the tip of the iceberg.' She paused a moment as the painful memories gripped her, twisting like a knife in her heart. She fixed her eyes on Bonnie, eyes that still glittered with unshed tears. 'I saw a kind, loving, gentle man turn into a monster.'

Bonnie's eyes turned in horror. 'Oh, Val, you don't mean . . .' she whispered.

Val waved a hand in the air. 'Oh, he never physically abused me or my mother. He just became more and more withdrawn, sullen, argumentative, depressed. Nothing pleased him. There was no way to reach him any more.' She leaned back in her chair with a sigh. 'In fact, I've often wondered if the accident wasn't deliberate, that he meant to kill them both. What's more, I don't think my mother even cared by then whether she lived or died.'

'I see,' Bonnie said slowly. 'And you ran away because you saw David turning into your father.'

Val nodded. 'Something like that. I realise now that what I did was wrong, that running away never really solves anything, but, Bonnie, it was such a nightmare!' She shuddered and raised her hands in a helpless gesture. 'I just couldn't cope.'

'I know,' Bonnie put in quickly. 'I do understand, Val, and I'm sorry I dragged it all up again this way. It's just that I hate to see the past keep you from——' She broke off and bit her lip, as though debating whether to go on, then took a deep breath and plunged ahead. 'Well, I'm wondering if maybe you're afraid to let a man get close to you just because of those two bad experiences with David and your father. Not all men are weak and unreliable, you know. Besides, you were only a girl then. Now you're a grown woman, after all, and it's not very bright to let the past spoil your whole life.'

'Oh, believe me, I've thought of that,' Val said with feeling. 'And you may be right.' She smiled. 'On the other hand, so far I really haven't met a man who appealed to me enough even to make me want to try to understand my own motives.'

'Does that include Michael Prescott?' Bonnie asked in a low voice.

Val shook her head firmly. 'You can forget about Michael Prescott. That's not on. He's gone. I'll never see him again.' She looked up to see the waitress heading in their direction with a loaded tray. 'Besides, he was a little too rich for my blood.' She shook out her napkin and spread it over her lap. 'Here comes our food. I'm starved.'

That night in her room as Val was packing her bags, that conversation with Bonnie played over and over again in her mind, like a broken record. Although she might have convinced her old friend that the subject of Michael was a dead issue, she still wasn't quite so sure of it herself.

Maybe Bonnie was right. Maybe she should have gone with him when he asked her. Had she refused because of outraged virtue, or, as Bonnie had suggested so bluntly, simply as a reaction against her old fears? She was very attracted to him, more than to any man she'd known since David. But she didn't quite trust him.

She sat down on the edge of the bed, her chin in her hand, staring down at the pattern in the carpet. The question was whether her suspicions were based on fact or fancy. Maybe she was right to suspect his motives. He had come on awfully strong, especially after such a bad beginning.

Yet, even now, her treacherous body still grew heated as she recalled how it felt to be in his arms, to feel his mouth on hers, his hands on her body...

She'd do it! What would she have to lose? She was twenty-eight years old. What did it matter that there were no guarantees? He may not be in love with her, but he certainly wanted her badly. And she wanted him. But how to contact him? She didn't even know where he was.

The card! She jumped up and ran to the waste-paper basket. There at the bottom, underneath a wad of Kleenex and the wrappings from a new pair of stockings, was a little pile of torn shreds. She scooped up as many as she could find, then went over to the dresser and laid the tiny pieces out on top. She'd just have to try to fit them together until she could make out the telephone number.

After puzzling over it for half an hour, she finally had to face the fact that it was an impossible task. She'd done too thorough a job on it, and none of the pieces seemed to fit. She could have cried with frustration.

Should she call his mother to get his number in Los Angeles? It seemed the only solution. She hated to do it, but what choice did she have? She swept the torn pieces of the card back into the waste-paper basket and walked slowly over to the telephone.

She had just reached for the receiver when it rang in her hand. She snatched it up, cursing the interruption. Now that she had herself all primed to call him, she didn't want to lose her nerve.

'Hello,' she said curtly.

'Val, it's Michael.'

She held in a breath, and for a moment her heart simply stopped beating. Then it began to thud erratically. She'd been so afraid she would never hear that voice again. Maybe he hadn't left town after all.

'Michael,' she said at last. 'Where are you?'

'I'm at my place in Los Angeles.'

Her spirits plummeted. 'I see,' she said.

'Since you haven't called, I gather you haven't changed your mind about coming down here to join me.'

Her mind raced. Should she or shouldn't she? Of course she should. She'd already decided that before he called. But before she could tell him so, he was speaking again.

'So, I decided that if the mountain wouldn't come to Mohammed . . .' He laughed drily. 'Well, you know the story. Anyway, I just wanted to make sure you hadn't already left for Seattle. I'm coming back to Carleton.'

She could hardly believe her ears. 'You're coming back here?'

'As soon as I can get a flight. Probably tomorrow morning.' There was a short silence, then he went on in a low voice, 'Will I be welcome? Or have I blown it by pushing too hard too soon?'

'I'll be very glad to see you again, Michael,' she said softly.

'Good. I'd leave tonight, but I still have a few things I have to take care of at the foundation tomorrow morning. I'll get away as soon as I can and take the first flight out.' He paused a moment. 'Maybe I could talk you into coming to the San Francisco airport to meet me.'

'You're not driving, then?'

'No. I flew down here and left my car at my mother's place.' He hesitated again. 'I could rent a car, I suppose.'

'No, don't do that. I don't mind coming to pick you up.'

'That's good.' He lowered his voice. 'Because the drive takes eight hours, and I'm in a hurry.'

CHAPTER SIX

EARLY the next morning, Val received a telephone call from Myra Barnes. When she heard her voice, she felt a swift stab of guilt. She'd promised to visit her again in the hospital, but had been so wrapped up in her own affairs that she'd forgotten all about it. The poor girl must be lonely stuck in that hospital bed, unable even to get around on her own.

'Thank goodness I've reached you at last,' Myra said. 'I've been trying to get hold of you for days, but you're never in.'

'I'm so sorry, Myra. You know how it is.' She laughed. 'This hotel room isn't a place I want to spend much time in. Besides, I've been pretty busy. You know, friends to see, a few trips into the city. Was there something special you wanted to talk to me about?'

'Yes. Yes, there is. Could you possibly come to see me some time today?'

Val glanced at her watch. It was nine o'clock. Michael had called before she was even dressed that morning to tell her he'd booked an eleven o'clock flight and that his plane would get into the San Francisco airport at noon.

That still left her an hour to kill before she had to leave. She definitely didn't want to have another little heart-to-heart talk with Bonnie, nor was she in the mood to tire herself out with another shopping expedition on the crowded city streets. She might as well go and see Myra. She'd promised her she would, after all, and it would be a real kindness.

'All right, Myra,' she said at last. 'There's something I have to do at ten o'clock, but I can stop by for a short visit on my way.'

As she drove the short distance to the hospital, she wondered what it was Myra was so anxious to talk to her about. Perhaps she'd decided to tell the Prescotts the truth about what had happened with David the night he was killed, that she herself had encouraged him to take that first fatal drink.

Although that was probably too much to hope for, it would certainly solve a major problem of her own by clearing the air and putting Michael's last lingering suspicions to rest.

As excited and relieved as she'd been after his unexpected call last night, there were still little doubts nagging at the back of her mind, doubts which all centred around David's death. The issue hung between them like a knife. They had skirted it many times, but always ended by backing away.

She was convinced that, if they were to have any kind of relationship at all, that problem had to be resolved. In at least some part of his mind, she knew that Michael still blamed her, or he wouldn't clam up and shy away from the subject every time it arose the way he did, even in casual conversation. And somehow Myra held the key.

Myra was alone in her room, lying on her side, her head turned towards the open door, her eyes closed. Her appearance was vastly improved since Val's first visit, her facial bruises fading, her general colour much better.

'Myra,' she called softly.

Myra opened her eyes. 'Oh, Val,' she said, struggling to sit up. 'I'm so glad you came.'

'Here, let me help you,' Val said, hurrying towards the bed.

'No need. I can do it.' Myra pressed a button and the head of the bed rose up gradually so that by the time Val reached her side she was already in a sitting position.

'Well, you're certainly looking well,' Val said, seating herself on the chair beside the bed.

'I feel a lot better, too, but the doctors say it'll be weeks before I'll really be back on my feet again.'

'I suppose that's to be expected with injuries as serious as yours.'

They chatted for a while about Myra's progress, then went on to discuss Val's job and her life in Seattle, but Myra didn't seem to be paying much attention to the conversation. She kept glancing out of the window, twisting the ties of her nightgown around her fingers, and when she spoke at all it was only in monosyllables.

In fact, now that Val was actually here, Myra was acting as though she could hardly wait until she left. She seemed so distracted and nervous that after a time Val began to suspect she was making these rather desperate attempts at small talk simply to avoid the real reason she'd called.

'Myra,' she said finally after another long pause, 'you said on the telephone that there's something you especially wanted to talk to me about. Maybe you'd better tell me what it is. I really do have to leave soon.'

The girl drew in a deep breath, and gave Val a troubled look. 'It's—it's about Michael Prescott,' she finally stammered out.

Val raised an eyebrow. 'Michael? What about him?'

'I've been lying here for days worrying over what he might do.'

'Do? What do you mean?'

'Do to you.'

Val could only stare. 'To me?' she asked slowly. 'What could he possibly do to me?' She smiled. 'He doesn't seem very dangerous.'

'Surely you know how furious he was at you, how convinced he was that it was all your fault, what happened to David?'

'Well, I think he did feel that way at first,' Val said carefully. 'But since then we've pretty much buried the hatchet. I don't believe he's still angry.'

Myra didn't look convinced. 'I hope you're right, but I've been worried to death that he'd do something really awful.'

'I don't understand,' Val said, puzzled. 'Like what?'

'He kept talking about paying you back for what you did to David. What he *thought* you did,' she amended hastily. 'I don't know. He seemed to have a real fixation about getting some kind of revenge.'

A cold chill gripped Val's heart. 'Revenge?' she said in a small voice. 'What kind of revenge?'

'Oh, something about showing you what it felt like to love someone and then get dumped. He even seemed to think that hurting you would somehow make it better for me, that he was doing it for my sake as well as his.'

'I see. I take it then that you haven't told him the truth about what really happened that night, that you know it had nothing to do with me.'

Myra shook her head. 'I can't. I'm sorry, Val, but I just can't do it. I couldn't bear it if he and his mother knew it was my fault David started drinking again.' Her lower lip began to quiver as her voice rose out of control.

'But it wasn't your fault,' Val said, leaning closer. 'I know David's mother. She knew what he was like.'

Myra was crying noisily by now, and Val realised it was hopeless to try to convince her. Maybe when Myra recovered all her strength she would find the courage to tell the truth. But by then it might be too late.

'Well, never mind,' Val said. 'It probably doesn't matter. Right now you should concentrate on getting well. And, as I said, whatever animosity Michael may have felt towards me before, it's all over now. Try to forget it.'

But later, after she'd left the hospital and was driving back to the hotel, Val found it wasn't that easy to forget. Had Michael's initial reaction to her really changed?

What if it hadn't? The small seed of suspicion she'd had about Michael's motives even before her talk with Myra began to sprout and grow. If it was true, if he had pursued her, wooed her, tried to seduce her, just to get revenge, it meant that everything that had happened between them was a lie.

Back in her room, she paced up and down, in an agony of indecision. She wanted desperately to go to him, to believe him, to follow her heart. Was she going to let one conversation with a virtual stranger resurrect her old fears and spoil everything just when she was so certain she'd grown out of them?

What had Myra actually said that was so terrible? She'd been worried because Michael was so resentful at what he imagined was her role in David's death. Well, that was nothing new, after all. She'd always known that. He'd made no secret of his anger. And as for his telling Myra he wanted to punish her in some way, at the time he'd been so distraught over his brother's death, he might have said anything.

The one thing she was certain of was that he couldn't possibly have faked his attraction to her. She knew genuine desire when she saw it. The way he looked at her, touched her, held her, that was real.

It was almost ten o'clock. If she was going to the airport to pick him up, she'd have to leave in a few minutes. She stopped short by the side of the bed. If she went, it would have to be because she trusted him, and that meant refusing to dwell on her suspicions.

She took a deep breath, grabbed her handbag off the bed, and hurried out into the corridor, locking the door behind her.

The minute she saw his tall figure striding towards her, all her reservations about him fled from her mind, and she realised that she was already half in love with him. It was too late to back down now.

'Hello, there,' he said when he reached her side. He put an arm casually around her shoulders. 'Glad you could make it.'

'I said I would,' she replied with a smile.

'I know. I guess I was afraid you'd change your mind.'

'Oh, no,' she said lightly. 'My word is my bond.'

He pulled her more tightly up against him. When she looked up at him, a lovely warmth flooded through her when she saw that, for the first time since she'd known him, the smile on his lips also lit up his brilliant blue eyes.

He felt it, too, she was certain, from the way his hand clenched on her shoulder, the way he searched her face, as though he'd been waiting for her all his life. And as he bent his head slowly towards her there was no mistaking his desire for her.

As they stood there in the busy airport terminal, the loudspeaker blaring, the people rushing past them, the sound of voices raised in greeting, it seemed to Val that they were actually all alone, that nothing else existed except the promise in his smile, his look, his touch.

Just then she was abruptly jostled from behind, and she turned around to see a woman who was trying to manage a large suitcase in one hand and a sobbing child in the other, looking harried and stammering out apologies.

The spell was broken, and with a rueful little laugh Michael dropped his arm from her shoulder.

'I think we're blocking traffic here,' he said. 'Shall we go?'

Outside they headed for her rental car, which she had parked in the car park in front of the terminal. When they reached it, Michael stowed his one small piece of luggage in the back, then shrugged out of his jacket and threw it casually on the seat.

'Would you like me to drive?' he asked.

'Please,' she said, reaching in her bag and handing him the keys.

Inside the car, he adjusted the seat to accommodate his long legs, checked out the instruments on the dashboard and put the key in the ignition. Then, before starting the engine, he shifted his body around so that he was facing her.

'Thanks again for coming, Val,' he said in a low voice. 'I was afraid I'd ruined everything.'

'No,' she said. 'You haven't.'

He reached out a hand and touched her hair, which she'd brushed out loosely to her shoulders. 'And thanks for wearing your hair that way.' He moved closer to her so that their bodies were touching and his eyes bored into hers. 'Was that for my benefit?'

'Yes,' she murmured, hypnotised by that steady blue gaze. 'Yes, it was.'

The hand moved underneath the soft fall of her hair now to run lightly along her cheek, her jawline, then slid around to the back of her neck. His eyes were half closed, his lips slightly parted. As Val gazed up at him, she felt a tightness in her throat, and when the pressure of his hand tightened, impelling her slowly forward, she sank towards him.

'Val,' he whispered.

His mouth came down on hers then, and the sweetness of his kiss pierced to her very heart. She *knew* he cared for her, felt something more for her than mere physical desire, and at that moment she would have followed him to the end of the earth.

They spoke very little on the drive. Val was content to sit close to his side, where he had firmly positioned her before starting off. Each time she felt the motion of his body as he shifted gears or braked or turned a corner, it felt as though an electric current were running through her.

When they reached the outskirts of Carleton and came to the side-road that led to his mother's house, he turned into it and started up the hill. 'It's almost two o'clock and I haven't had any lunch yet. How about you? Are you hungry?'

It occurred to her then that she hadn't eaten since her meagre breakfast several hours ago. 'Well, yes,' she replied. 'As a matter of fact, I am.'

'We can probably find something to eat at the house. My mother is the old-fashioned kind who always keeps a virtual grocery store of her own stocked in the kitchen.'

Although Val was pleased at the thought of seeing Mrs Prescott again, she couldn't help feeling a little stab of disappointment. She had hoped they could be alone.

'Won't she object to an unexpected guest?' she asked lightly.

They had reached the top of the rise now. Michael pulled the car in under the acacia tree in front of the house, but left the motor idling. He sat very still staring fixedly through the front windscreen for several moments, a slight frown on his face. Then he turned to her.

'I think I should tell you,' he said carefully, 'that my mother isn't here. She's visiting her sister in Santa Rosa for a few days.'

'I see.'

His meaning was perfectly clear. He was telling her that they would have the house to themselves, be all alone, after all. In an oblique, round-about way, he was making his intentions clear, and at the same time giving her the chance to think it over, to back out before she committed herself irrevocably.

She didn't even hesitate. She was already committed. There was no turning back now. She couldn't have gone off with him to Los Angeles when he'd asked her to, but the fact that he was able to rise above his own ego and come back for her proved to her that she was important to him.

She met his gaze. 'I'll be sorry to miss her,' she said evenly.

Immediately the frown lines on his face smoothed, and the look of sheer relief on his face told her all she needed to know. He wasn't like the other men she'd known, who vanished the moment she made it clear to them that hopping into bed was not her idea of appropriate behaviour for a casual acquaintance.

There was nothing casual about her relationship with Michael—hadn't been from the very beginning. Even when they had seemed to be enemies, she'd sensed that there was more substance to him, more sensitivity.

'Well, then,' he said, 'let's go inside.'

The house was cool and dim, with all the curtains and draperies drawn against the afternoon sun. They made straight for the large, friendly kitchen, which was very quiet, except for the ticking of the clock on the wall over the counter.

Michael went directly to the refrigerator, opened the door and peered inside, while Val set her bag down on the wooden table in the centre of the room and stood there watching him. Now that her mind was made up, she couldn't get enough of his tall, graceful form as he bent over to rummage around inside. His every motion sent a thrill of delicious anticipation running through her.

'Do you want to come and take a look?' he called to her over his shoulder. 'There's enough food in here to feed an army. I see ham, a bowl of chicken salad, plenty of fruit and at least three different kinds of cheese.'

She walked over to his side and gazed down at his dark head. For the first time she noticed that he had a rather unruly cowlick at the crown where the thick strands of black hair parted, and that there were some faint silver threads almost buried among them.

He stood up and turned to her. They weren't quite touching, although they were so close now that she could sense the warmth of his skin, see the little pulse beating at the base of his tanned throat where he had loosened his tie and undone the top button of his white shirt.

Their eyes met. The smile on his face faded. He leaned forward slightly so that their bodies just barely met. The spark generated by that touch was all it took. He reached out for her and she fell into his embrace with a sigh.

She raised her arms up around his neck, holding him as tightly as he held her, and they stood there locked together for several long, delicious moments. His mouth was at her ear, and she could hear the rasp of his laboured breathing.

'Val,' he murmured huskily. 'Oh, Val.'

He lifted his head and gave her one long, penetrating look, then, with his lips parted, his mouth came down hard on hers, hungry, greedy. This time there was no holding back, no resistance, and she responded to the hot mouth, the probing tongue with every fibre of her being.

So this was what it was like, she thought as she savoured the taste of his mouth, the scent of his skin. This is what I've been missing, longing for for all these years.

'I want you, Val,' he murmured against her lips.

She placed her hand on his cheek and ran it over the rough stubble of his jaw. 'Yes, Michael,' she said. 'I know.'

In a soft, caressing motion he pulled the straps of her sun-dress down over her arms, then leaned over to press his lips against her bare shoulder. She shivered as his hands moved up and down over her skin, and he drew her closer.

'Are you cold?' he asked huskily. Wordlessly, she shook her head. Without taking his eyes from hers, he slowly unbuttoned his shirt and dropped it on the floor. 'Touch me,' he whispered.

She reached out tentatively, shyly, and placed one hand on his smooth chest. At the first touch of the hot, firm flesh, the hard muscles underneath, she uttered a low cry, pressed herself against him and slid her arms back up around his neck.

He kissed her again and ran his hands down her back, clutching at her hips and pulling her lower body tightly against his hard need. His lips left hers and moved to her neck, her shoulders, the ridge of her collarbone, and finally came to her breast. With his tongue, he made circles around the soft fullness, until his mouth closed eagerly over first one hard, thrusting peak, then the other.

Val threw her head back in an unconscious gesture of total surrender to the thrilling sensations that filled her whole being, mind and body, and when he undid the zip of her dress and knelt before her to pull it to the floor there was no thought of stopping him. As he rose up to his feet, his hands moved slowly over her legs and hips to settle possessively once more over her breasts.

Then, in one swift movement, he scooped her up in his arms and carried her down the hallway to the open door of a bedroom. Still holding her, he stood at the side of the bed for a moment, and when he spoke his voice was gentle.

'Are you sure, Val?' he asked softly.

She ran her fingers through the crisp, thick hair. 'Yes,' she said quietly. 'I'm sure.'

Carefully, he laid her down on top of the bed, and she watched as he slipped out of his remaining clothing. Val had never seen a naked man before, and she was struck by the hardness of his sinewy muscles and the tall strength of his body, so different from her own.

He lay down, hovering over her for a moment, staring down at her and moving a hand over her face as though to memorise it. His mobile mouth came down on hers, seeking and probing, and as his lips and hands began to work their magic on her body once again she sank back on the pillow and simply followed her own instincts.

Finally, when the aching desire had become almost painful, his body came to cover hers at last, and she breathed a low sigh of satisfaction. After one sharp jab of pain came the mounting sensations of pleasure, and at the last, with his hoarse cry filling her ears, wave after wave of ecstatic release came flooding through her, and for the first time in her life Val knew at last the full measure of a man's love.

It was dark when Val woke up. For a moment she was disorientated and couldn't imagine where she was. She opened her eyes and gazed around the unfamiliar room. It was almost dark now, but it looked to be a very spare, very masculine bedroom.

Then she glanced over at the sleeping man by her side, and a flood of warmth glowed within her. He was lying on his stomach, facing away from her, the thin covers rumpled around his waist, leaving his bare, broad shoulders and strong back visible. It was all she could do to keep from reaching out and stroking her hand down that long sweep of tanned flesh, but she decided to let him sleep.

She wanted to savour the lovely moments they'd had together all by herself for a while. Besides that, her stomach felt as though it hadn't been fed for a week. All she'd had that day was breakfast, and she'd been so excited then about the prospect of seeing Michael again that she'd hardly touched it.

Slowly and carefully, so as not to disturb him, she eased herself off the bed. Somehow it didn't seem right to her to wander through Mrs Prescott's house stark naked, and she groped on the floor for some article of the clothing she had discarded so frantically just a few hours ago.

She finally found her slip. Pulling it over her head, she tiptoed out of the room and made for the kitchen. She switched on the overhead light and saw by the clock still ticking on the wall that it was past nine o'clock. No wonder she was so starved. She went over to the fridge, took out the bowl of chicken salad and set it on the table.

On her way to the cupboard for silverware and a plate, she noticed the shirt Michael had dropped on the floor earlier in such a hurry. Smiling secretly to herself, she reached down to pick it up. On an impulse, she raised it to her face and pressed her cheek against its smooth texture, drinking in the lingering scent that was uniquely his.

She shook it out gently to smooth the wrinkles, and as she did so an envelope fell out of the breast pocket. After retrieving it from the floor, she glanced idly at it before putting it back. When she saw the return address, her eyes widened. It was from the university hospital in Seattle.

She stood there for several moments, torn between the temptation to open it and the knowledge that it would be wrong to pry. Finally she compromised by holding it up to the light. It was only one short typewritten paragraph, clearly legible through the thin envelope.

As she read it her eyes swam, her head reeled, and she felt as though she were teetering on the edge of a precipice. It was from the chief of staff of the cardiac centre, briefly acknowledging Michael's acceptance of their offer. It was dated the twenty-eighth of July, three weeks ago.

Still holding the letter, she sank weakly into a nearby chair. Three weeks ago! That was before she'd even met him. She stared blindly at the bowl of chicken salad, her appetite gone, a knot of fear twisting in her stomach.

Gradually, the fear turned to anger. He'd lied to her about the Seattle job! He'd told her he hadn't yet made up his mind whether to accept it. But why? Why lie about a thing like that? What difference could it make?

There could only be one reason. He'd never had any intention of pursuing the relationship beyond a quick seduction, not the first time he'd told her about the Seattle offer, not later on when she'd finally gathered the courage to ask him about it point-blank. And not this afternoon, either.

Gradually the anger exploded into a red-hot fury. She stuffed the letter back in his shirt pocket and dropped it on the floor, then jumped up and started pacing around the room, wringing her hands and groaning aloud. If he'd lied about that, he'd probably lied about other things, too. Oh, God, what had she done?

She had to think. This was no time to fall to pieces. As she grew calmer, she suddenly recalled Myra's warnings just that very morning, her fears about what Michael might do to get revenge for his brother's death. At the time she'd rejected them, convinced that her previous suspicions about the abrupt change in his attitude towards her were merely her old paranoia at work. Now it all fitted together.

All she could think of now was to get away, out of that house, as far away from Michael Prescott as she could get. But she couldn't go back into that bedroom where he still lay sleeping. Not unless she wanted to murder him in his bed! Which was exactly what she felt like doing at that moment.

She switched off the overhead light and groped her way to the back door, then stumbled out into the small garden. It was a warm, balmy summer evening, but she stood there shivering uncontrollably in her thin slip. She buried her face in her hands, digging her fists into her eyes as an intense feeling of sorrow swept over her.

She'd actually been in love with him! She'd trusted him, believed he cared about her. Once again, the old pattern of betrayal had worked against her. It would never end. Somehow she seemed to be fated to love only men who would hurt her. First her father, then David, now his brother.

Her immediate problem, however, was how to get away without waking him. The one thing she wanted to avoid was a scene with him. There was no telling what she might do or say. She'd have to go back into that bedroom to collect her clothes and find the keys to her rental car.

Just then she saw the kitchen light go on, heard the door open and close, footsteps. It was too late. He was already walking slowly towards her, wearing only his dark trousers, his chest and arms bare. She turned away from him, gritting her teeth, steeling herself for what she knew was ahead.

'There you are,' he said softly as he came up behind her.

He put his arms around her, pressing his face against hers, his body warm on her back. Then, when both hands settled on her breasts, to her horror she felt herself responding to his touch.

She stiffened, pulled herself free and moved away from him. When she turned around to face him, there was a puzzled look on his face.

'Val,' he said, taking a step towards her. 'What is it?'

'Why didn't you tell me you'd already accepted the job in Seattle?' she asked in a flat, accusing tone.

He only gazed blankly at her for several long seconds. Then he ran his fingers through his hair and stared down at his feet. When he raised his head to face her again, his eyes were cold, his jaw clenched.

'How did you find out?' he asked in a tight monotone. Then he nodded briefly. 'You found the letter.'

Val waved a hand in the air. 'It doesn't matter.' She raised her chin. 'You lied to me, Michael. Why?'

He crossed his arms over his chest and cocked his head to one side. 'I was going to tell you today, but——' He broke off with a shrug. 'We got sidetracked.'

Val's face went up in flame at the memory of just what it was that had distracted him. If indeed he had been planning to tell her at all, which she seriously doubted.

'Then you admit you lied to me,' she bit out.

'Yes. I admit it. But that was before——'

'Before what?' she cried. 'Before your little plan worked and you succeeded in getting me into bed with you!'

He frowned and reached out a hand. 'Now, listen, Val, what happened between us had nothing to do with it. What's more, you wanted it as badly as I did.'

'And just what other little lies and deceptions have you practised on me?' she challenged. 'Myra warned me about your clever scheme to get revenge for what you thought I did to David.' She laughed harshly. 'I didn't believe her at the time, but now it makes perfect sense.'

In her heart of hearts, Val knew that even now she was still hoping that somehow he could explain the letter and brush off Myra's vendetta theory so that she could believe him. She wanted to believe him, more than anything else in the world. But he only stood there, his face a blank mask.

Finally, his shoulders slumped forwards and he heaved a deep sigh. 'All right, Val. I admit that, too. It was on my mind at the beginning to, well, pay you back for hurting David the way you did. The way I thought you did,' he amended hastily. 'You were right. It was going to be just a quick seduction. I lied to you about having already accepted the post in Seattle because I never wanted us to meet again when it was over, and I couldn't have you knowing I'd soon be living in the same city.'

'So it *was* all an act,' she said through her teeth. 'Tracking me down in the hotel to apologise, the day at Marsh Creek, the sexy come-on at dinner, and . . .' Her voice faltered, and she turned her head away, unable to look at him. 'And what happened today.'

'No!' he shouted. He gripped her hard by the shoulders and forced her around to face him. 'Not today,' he said in a softer tone.

She gazed up at him, searching his face. His eyes glittered in the light from inside the house; his jaw was hard and set. He looked as though he meant it. Was it just another act? He'd taken her in once. Why shouldn't he be able to do it again?

'I don't believe you,' she said flatly.

'I changed my mind about you days ago,' he said. 'And I came back because I wanted to see you again, wanted to be with you.' He searched her face. 'Val? You've got to believe me.'

She wanted to. In a way she did. But everything was spoiled for her now. It had cost her so much to trust him, to put aside her old fears. Now, with his admission that he had indeed deceived her from the very beginning, taken her in, in spite of her caution, her reservations about his motives, how could she ever trust him again? More to the point, how could she trust herself?

Even if he were telling her the truth now, what kind of future was he offering her? Their whole relationship was haunted by the spectre of David's death. It would always be an obstacle between them. She had to be strong enough to give him up now, before he really broke her heart.

'I'm sorry, Michael,' she said at last. 'It's just not going to work.'

He dropped his hands from her shoulders. 'Val, what can I say? I was wrong, I admit it. How can I make it up to you?'

Even then, she thought, if he'd only say one word, tell her he loved her, make her even the faintest of promises, she knew she would have weakened. But he only stood there, proud and tall, waiting for *her* surrender.

She shook her head sadly. 'Well, you got what you wanted,' she said. 'I hope it was worth it.'

'Val, if you'd just listen to reason . . .'

She knew if she stayed there one more second she would start to cry. She couldn't give him that satisfaction, too. He'd already taken so much from her, and she needed whatever vestige of her tattered pride she could cling to.

'I'm going to get dressed now,' she said shakily. 'Then I'm going to leave. But before I do, I just want to say one thing to you. I may have treated David badly. Perhaps I was even partly responsible for what happened to him. But I think you were at least as much to blame as I was.'

He blanched then, as though she had struck him, the colour draining from his face, and for one moment she regretted her harsh, hurtful words. It was all she could do to keep from reaching out to him, and only the swift reminder of what he had done to her stopped her in time.

There was nothing more to say. With her head held high, she walked stiffly past him, and went directly back to the bedroom, averting her eyes from the bed where only hours before she had lain with him in such transports of ecstasy.

CHAPTER SEVEN

ONE grey, drizzly morning, a week after her hurried flight away from Carleton, Val left the tall condominium at the top of Queen Anne Hill where she lived, walked to the corner and took the regular bus into the Seattle city centre.

She'd spent that week in a frenzy of activity, anything to keep her mind occupied and off that humiliating experience with Michael Prescott. If she gave herself any time at all to think, she would inevitably find herself replaying the whole ugly scenario once again, leaving her trembling with rage and shame.

Now, with every inch of the small condo unit cleaned and scrubbed, the kitchen painted a bright cheerful yellow against Seattle's dreary winters, all the curtains freshly laundered and rehung, every stitch of clothing mended and pressed, and long-delayed letters written, she'd simply run out of things to do, and it felt as though the walls were closing in on her.

She got off the bus in front of the Rainier Building on Fifth Avenue, where the boutique was located, and walked quickly through a gusty shower through the revolving door into the atrium, then climbed the stairs to the second level, taking off her headscarf and shaking it out as she went.

As she passed by the small leather goods shop, the book store, the confectioner's, she took her key out of her bag. It was nine-thirty. The shop opened at ten o'clock, and she wasn't sure whether Janet, her assistant, would be there yet to get ready for the day's rush of business. The shop was very popular with the downtown professional women and society matrons who came into the city from the sprawling suburbs to shop.

Heading towards the front door, she glanced at the window display with a critical eye. Janet had done a good job, just the right juxtaposition of an expensive black knit suit in elegant good taste with a brightly patterned silk scarf and chunky gold jewellery to give the sober suit an added zing.

She unlocked the door and stepped inside. Janet was behind the counter folding a new shipment of cashmere sweaters. As Val walked towards her, she raised her eyes and stared blankly.

'What in the world are you doing here?' she asked. 'You still have another few days of vacation.'

'Oh, I decided to save it for later on in the winter,' Val replied in an offhand tone. 'I thought I might try a skiing trip to Aspen this year.'

'You don't ski.'

'Well, I can always learn, can't I?'

She shrugged out of her raincoat and went into the back room to hang it up. Janet followed her and stood in the doorway watching her with a puzzled expression on her round, plump face.

'I don't get it,' she said at last. 'You were so looking forward to your trip, seeing your old friends again at the reunion.' She hesitated for a moment, then said, 'Did something happen?'

Val turned around to face her. 'Yes, as a matter of fact,' she said briskly, 'something did. The boy—the man, actually—I especially went down there to see was killed in an accident the night of the big party.'

She shrugged. 'That pretty much put a damper on any celebration, so there didn't seem to be much point in my hanging around. Besides, I'd already seen everyone I really wanted to.'

'Gosh, Val, that's a shame,' Janet said. 'I'm sorry your trip had to be spoiled likc that.' Then she brightened. 'Well, anyway, it's good to have you back. The temporary clerk we hired hasn't turned out to be worth a darn, and I've been run off my feet. You know what it's like every year the minute we start putting out the new fall lines.'

Val smiled. 'Speaking of that, while I was in California, I went into San Francisco on a scouting trip one day and came across a wonderful new designing house. I gave them a small order to see how well it's received up here, but I think it's a winner.'

It was so good to be back at work, she thought, as she went on to describe the new items she'd ordered. In time she would forget all about Michael Prescott and that whole disastrous trip.

The weather deteriorated steadily all through September, with dense fogs in the morning followed inevitably by rain in the afternoon. Ordinarily Val enjoyed the wet bleak autumns that other people, especially Californians, found so depressing, but this year seemed to be different.

She was fine as long as she was at the shop working, and in the evenings she was always too tired after her ten-hour day to do much more than read the paper, watch a little television, clean up and get her clothes ready for work the next day.

It was the weekends that were so difficult. With the almost constant rain, she was pretty much housebound, and, although hardier souls still jogged or trudged along the footpath around Green Lake in the heart of the city, Val couldn't quite work up the energy or enthusiasm to join them.

She found herself on Saturdays and Sundays sitting in her living-room and staring blankly out of the window at the view of the city and the harbour that she used to find so fascinating. In spite of all her efforts, her thoughts inevitably seemed to turn to that last day with Michael, reliving the whole thing over and over again in her mind.

The worst of it was that she always ended by wondering if she'd been too hasty in her judgement of him. There was no escaping the fact that when she had confronted him with his lies, his deceptions, he had seemed genuinely sorry. He had admitted everything, even tried to persuade her he had changed his mind, that he wanted to continue the relationship.

But he *had* deceived her, after all, she would console herself. He had deliberately set out to seduce her just for the sake of some stupid childish revenge. The trouble was, he had succeeded only too well. Since she'd been home she had reluctantly accepted a few dinner invitations from men she'd gone out with in the past, but by the end of the evening she always found herself measuring them against the one man who had penetrated past her defences.

Had she made a terrible mistake to stalk off the way she had? It was too late to worry about that now. She had no choice but to get him out of her mind and heart.

During the first week of October there came a spell of Indian summer, with crisp, clear sunny days and blue skies, and Val resumed her walks around the lake. Even though she knew the balmy weather would be short-lived, the physical activity was still good for her. At the very least, it tired her out so that she was sleeping better.

Then, one afternoon while she was in the front of the shop straightening out the debris left by the noontime rush, she heard Janet call her name from the back room where she was eating her lunch.

Val went to the open doorway and looked inside. Janet was sitting at the long wooden work table, a sandwich in one hand, the morning newspaper in the other.

'Hey, Val, take a look at this.' She held out the paper. 'Looks like your home town has made the news. Carleton, wasn't that where you went for your reunion?'

Puzzled as to how any news from Carleton could have reached the Seattle papers, Val took the page from Janet and scanned it briefly. When she saw the familiar face staring up at her, her heart skipped a beat, fluttered for a moment, then began to thud erratically.

The bold print beside the photograph read, 'Prominent California Physician to Head New University Cardiac Centre.' There was a short paragraph below. 'Michael Prescott has been named Chief of Staff of the new cardiac centre recently constructed at the university hospital.' It went on to describe the function of the centre, and ended with the sentence, 'Dr Prescott, a native of Carleton, California, has recently distinguished himself at the Richardson Cardiac Foundation in Los Angeles and will start his new position next week.'

Val raised the paper up in front of her face to hide the dismay she knew must be visible there. She'd known he had taken the job. Why should she be so shocked to read about it? She glanced at the photograph again. It was grainy, but there was no mistaking the proud lift of his head, the thick thatch of dark hair, and even in black and white the bright blue eyes seemed to glow.

It was a candid shot, rather than a studio portrait. He was standing at the window of what appeared to be a large office, apparently during an interview with the reporter. He had a hand raised in the air as though he was explaining something. The expression on his face was serious. He looked perfectly at ease, authoritative, secure in his lofty position.

'How about that?' Janet was saying. 'He looks pretty dishy. Did you know him?'

Val lowered the paper and handed it back to Janet. 'Only briefly and not very well,' she replied curtly. 'He was some years ahead of me in school.'

After that, Val's hard-won peace of mind was shattered. It was one thing to think of him as a distant fading memory, miles away in California, but to know he was now living and working right here in the same town was more than she could bear.

In spite of its large and growing population and metropolitan atmosphere, Seattle was a small town in many ways. In the days that followed, Val constantly imagined that she saw him, in every tall, dark man who crossed her path, or even at a distance. She was terrified that she would run into him, on the streets, in a restaurant or a shop.

But it never turned out to be Michael, and after a few weeks she began to sink back into her old pattern of dull despair. It was almost November, and the autumn storms had begun in earnest now, confining her once again either to her own four walls or the small shop, and she worked extra long hours, with frantic energy.

'Are you OK?' Janet asked her one morning in a troubled voice.

Val gave her a swift look. 'Of course. Why do you ask?'

Janet shrugged. 'Oh, I don't know. Ever since you came back from your vacation you've seemed different somehow. Distracted. And you look as though you've lost weight.'

'I've had a lot on my mind. You can't imagine all the problems involved in running a successful business.' Then, when she saw Janet's face fall, she added hastily, 'You're a big help to me, Janet, and I don't mean to belittle your part in making things work smoothly around here, but the major responsibility is mine, and, as I say, there are a lot of problems you're not even aware of.'

They were in the back room unpacking the shipment of the new line Val had ordered from San Francisco. Now that it had arrived, she was having second thoughts about the wisdom of her choice. What seemed so wonderful on a sunny day in California didn't look very marketable in Seattle in late October.

'I don't know, Janet,' Val said as she shook out a heavy white piqué dress and held it up. 'What do you think?'

Janet eyed it dubiously. 'Well, we could always save it for spring.'

'No,' Val said with quick decisiveness. 'I don't want to do that. We'll try a resort display, call it "Styles for the Sunny South" or something.'

Janet brightened. 'That's a marvellous idea. All of Seattle society migrates south after Christmas anyway.' She laughed. 'Although I'll bet you could come up with a better title.'

Val shrugged. 'Well, there are a few problems to iron out, I'll have to admit.'

Just then the front door opened and closed. Janet went over to the door and peered into the front of the shop. Groaning slightly under her breath, she turned and gave Val a disgusted look.

'Speaking of problems,' she said, 'one of our major examples just walked in the door.'

Val raised an eyebrow. 'Which one?' she asked drily. 'We have so many.'

'Diana Worth.'

Val laughed. 'Do you want me to tackle her?'

'Maybe you'd better. If she tries to return one more thing that she's already worn five times I'm afraid I'll throw it back in her face.'

'OK, but you owe me one. You can finish unpacking and start pressing.'

She went out into the front of the shop and walked slowly towards the tall, elegantly dressed blonde woman standing beside the counter. She was pawing through a display of costume jewellery it had taken Janet an hour to arrange just that morning.

'Good morning, Mrs Worth,' Val said. 'Can I help you with something today?'

The woman raised her perfectly styled blonde head and gave Val an artificial smile that was both placating and patronising at the same time. 'This stuff is terribly over-priced,' she said, dropping an amber bracelet back in the tray.

'Oh, do you think so?' Val replied pleasantly. 'Actually, it's sold rather well.'

She went over to the counter and began to rearrange the pieces back in their original order, all the while keeping one eye on Diana Worth, who was prowling around the shop, poking and tugging at the merchandise.

'Is there anything special you're looking for?' Val asked politely when she'd finished.

'Yes, as a matter of fact. There is.' She handed Val one of the shop's elegant pink bags, which was now torn and wrinkled. 'I'm returning this blouse. It has a flaw in it.'

'Really?' Val said smoothly, taking the parcel from her. 'Let me take a look.'

She laid the bag on the counter, reached inside and pulled out a pale blue silk blouse, one of the most expensive ones the shop carried. It had been folded haphazardly and stuffed in the bag any which way.

Val shook out the blouse and began to examine it carefully. It was a far cry from the lovely garment that had been sold originally. To her practised eye it was clear the blouse had been worn, not once, but several times. The seams under the arms were strained, there was a light film of grime at the back of the neck, and a faint pink stain on the left side of the collar, which looked suspiciously like a smudge of lipstick.

In the meantime, Diana Worth stood there watching her, tapping her foot impatiently and smoking a cigarette, right next to the discreet 'No Smoking' sign on the counter.

Val pointed to the stain. 'Is this the flaw you mentioned?' she asked.

'Yes. That's it. I'm afraid I didn't notice it until I wore it once, but you can see that I can't possibly keep it. You'll just have to take it back.'

Val turned her head slowly and looked directly into the pale grey eyes. She knew she'd have to take the blouse back, that was the shop's policy, and in spite of her machinations Diana Worth did spend a great deal of money there. She also wielded enormous power in her social circle. One disgruntled word from her, and Val could very well lose several valued customers.

Still, Val wanted the woman to know that she wasn't taken in by the lie. Their gaze held for a few long seconds. The haughty look on the blonde's face began to fade, the arrogant shoulders slumped a little and she had the grace to blush lightly.

Val smiled. She'd won her point. 'Of course we'll take it back, Mrs Worth,' she said graciously. 'You know our policy. Now, is there anything else I can help you with?'

The blonde frowned and glanced down at her watch. 'I'd like to try on that red dress in the window, but I'm meeting a friend for lunch and don't know if I have time.'

'Would you like me to set it aside for you? Then you can come back and try it on after you've had lunch.'

'No. I'll try it on now,' was the firm reply. She gave Val a knowing smile. 'It never hurts to make a man wait for you.'

Val ushered Diana into a dressing room, then got the red dress from the window and took it in to her.

While Diana undressed, Val undid the fastenings on the dress, and had just slipped it carefully over the blonde head when she heard someone come in the front door.

'Can you manage the rest of this by yourself?' she asked. 'I'll just be a minute.'

She left the dressing-room and went back out into the shop, a welcoming smile on her face. But the moment she laid eyes on the tall man who had just entered, the smile faded. It was Michael Prescott, the last man on earth she ever wanted to see again.

All the breath suddenly seemed to be knocked out of her. She stood stock-still, staring at him, unable to quite grasp the fact that he was really there. There was a strange pounding, roaring sensation in her ears, her knees grew weak, and for a moment she couldn't even remember where she was.

He was standing at the counter looking at the amber jewellery display. Although he was turned away from her, enough of his profile was showing so that she knew that this time there was no mistake. It really was him. But what in the world was he doing here? Had he tracked her down again? No, of course not. He detested her.

Her first instinct was to run. He hadn't seen her yet. He probably had no idea this was her shop. But while she hesitated, he suddenly turned around and they came face to face. His eyes widened fractionally and a slight pinkish flush washed over his face, but if he was taken off guard he recovered quickly.

They stared wordlessly at each other for several long moments. Then, finally, he spoke.

'Hello, Val,' he said quietly.

He started walking slowly towards her, but just then Diana suddenly emerged from the dressing-room with her head twisted around and both hands clutching at the back of the red dress.

'I need your help with this hook,' she said impatiently. Then she turned her head, and her eyes flicked from Michael to Val, then back to Michael again. 'Oh, Michael, darling,' she cried. 'I'm sorry if I kept you waiting.' She pirouetted gracefully on her high heels. 'How do you like the dress? Do you think the colour suits me?'

Michael gave her a long, sober, appraising look, then nodded. 'Very nice,' he said politely.

Relieved at the interruption, Val hung back and stayed there beside the counter, still shaky, watching the little scene, as Diana chattered on about the colour, the style, the fit, claiming all of Michael's attention.

She simply couldn't take her eyes off him. This man's presence was all she could think of. Those were the arms that held me, that was the mouth that kissed me, this is the body that lay against mine.

Gradually, her head began to clear and she slowly recovered her composure. It was only the shock of seeing him simply *appear* like that out of thin air, just when she thought she'd finally got him out of her system. Now she was able to watch him more calmly as he listened to Diana ramble on about her dress.

His expression was grave, attentive, courteous, giving away nothing. He looked tired, Val thought, the lines running down along from his straight nose alongside his mouth deeply etched, the blue eyes dimmed.

Now that Diana had distracted him with her fashion show and they were ignoring her, Val saw her chance to get out of there. She slipped behind the counter and quickly and quietly made her way into the back room, where Janet was still unpacking boxes.

'Janet, will you go on out there and finish up with Diana Worth?' she said in a low voice.

'Huh!' Janet snorted. 'I see she got to you, too.' She sighed. 'OK. What's the problem this time?'

'No problem. I've already taken care of it. She's just having a little trouble making up her mind about that red wool in the window, and you can stand around out there while she admires herself as well as I can. I'd really like to make a final decision about this new shipment before we unpack the whole thing.'

When Janet was gone, Val sat down at the table, folded her hands in front of her and closed her eyes. From the front of the shop the voices of the others drifted back, low murmurs, one masculine, punctuated by Diana's shrill, demanding tones.

What was he thinking? Val couldn't even begin to guess. Except for that first shock of recognition in his eyes, swiftly concealed, his face had been an expressionless mask. Somehow seeing him like this, so unexpectedly, seemed to have evaporated all her anger and resentment at the trick he'd played on her.

How did he feel about her? There was no way to tell. She recalled her parting words to him, bitter words, the accusation that he himself was to blame for his brother's death. He must hate her.

She couldn't really blame him. Not only had she wounded his masculine ego by walking out on him the way she did, but her parting shot must have hit a sore spot. She'd been wrong to accuse him of being responsible for David's death, but at the time she'd been suffering the pangs of her own guilt, and furious at his deception, still smarting at the way he'd seduced her into trusting him, believing he cared about her, just to wage his war of revenge.

She half rose out of her chair, filled with the sudden overpowering impulse to run out into the shop and tell him she was sorry. He had suffered, too. Perhaps he had behaved badly to her with his silly vendetta plan, but he was basically a decent person, and he *had* changed his mind. After all that had happened, they probably could never be friends, but she didn't want him for an enemy.

Then she sank slowly back down. What could she possibly accomplish? He was obviously involved with Diana Worth. Their brief encounter back in Carleton had no real significance for him. It had merely been the result of shock over David's death.

It was too late now anyway. He would never forgive her for those last parting words. She heard the front door open and close, then silence, and in a few minutes Janet stuck her head in the doorway. She made a face at Val.

'Well, she bought the dress. How much do you want to bet it comes back next week with a "flaw"?'

Val forced out at tight smile. 'Chalk it up to overheads. She may be a dud herself, but she does bring in a lot of good business.'

'Oh, I suppose so. I'll give her credit for one thing—she always manages to snag the greatest men. This latest one is the best of the lot. I wonder who he is.'

Val murmured something non-committal and got up from her chair to move another box on top of the table.

'He looked vaguely familiar,' Janet went on. 'I've been trying to think of where I've seen him before.'

Then she brightened. 'Now I remember. It was in the newspaper. The dishy doctor from your home town. He's even more devastating in person.'

Val busied herself unpacking the box, keeping her head averted, saying nothing. She could feel Janet's eyes boring into her, however, and finally had to look up.

'Well?' Janet said suggestively.

'Well, what?'

'Did you speak to him? I mean, talk over old times?'

Val yanked impatiently at the packing tape, breaking a fingernail in the process. 'Oh, Janet, I already told you,' she said sharply. 'We hardly knew each other. And it's been ten years.'

'I just thought you might have seen him on your vacation, that's all,' Janet said in a hurt voice.

Just then the telephone rang. With a sigh of relief, Val ran over to the desk and snatched up the receiver.

'Seattle Boutique,' she said. 'May I help you?'

'Val,' came a man's voice. 'Hi. It's Don Carter.'

'Oh, hello, Don,' she said. For just one moment, she'd thought he might be someone else. 'How are you?'

'Great. How about yourself? How was the vacation?'

'It was fine.'

Don Carter was a good-looking young man about town, one of the many Val had fended off not too delicately in the past. It had been months since he'd last called her. In fact, after their last wrestling match she'd expected never to hear from him again.

'The reason I'm calling,' he went on, 'is to ask you to go with me this Saturday night to a reception for my grandfather. He's finally retiring as Chairman of the Board of his bank. It'll be a rather boring affair, I'm afraid, but I would like to see you again if you can make it.' He gave a low chuckle. 'Besides, I need a favour from him and want to make a good impression on him, so I'm inviting the prettiest girl I know.'

Hah! Val snorted to herself. Fat chance of that! If it was a boring business affair, she knew darned well that he'd never be able to rope in any of the society debs he ordinarily squired around town.

'Sorry, Don,' she said cheerfully. 'Can't make it.'

'Oh, come on, Val,' he wheeled. 'Be a sport. I have to show up, it's a command performance, especially since I'm hoping to talk the old boy into floating me a loan for my new business venture, but we don't need to stay for the speeches. There'll be all the champagne you can drink and lots of goodies to eat. Won't you change your mind?'

Val sighed at the thought of another one of his silly, ill-fated business schemes. 'Afraid not,' she said in a tone of utter finality. 'But thanks for asking me.'

After they hung up, Val went back to the work table. Janet was still standing there and staring at her now with a decidedly critical look on her face.

'What was that all about?' she asked.

'Oh, it was only Don Carter. He wanted me to go to some dreary business affair with him Saturday night.'

'Don't you want to go? Or are you busy?'

'No, I'm not busy, but knowing Don I was his last resort, and I don't much like that. Besides, the last time I went out with him I spent half the night beating him off.'

'Val,' Janet said gravely, 'I think you should go.'

Val stared at her. 'Why in the world do you think that?'

Janet raised her chin and gave her a defiant look. 'Listen, I know you don't like people butting into your business, but we're friends, after all, and I really have to get this off my chest.'

'All right,' Val said slowly. 'Then you'd better go ahead and do it.'

Janet took a deep breath. 'Ever since you came back from your vacation, you've been in virtual hibernation, and I think it's time you snapped out of it and started getting out and around again. What difference does it make that Don Carter is something of a creep? Who knows? You might meet someone interesting through him.'

Val opened her mouth and gave her a warning look, but Janet only set her lips in a determined line and raised a hand to forestall her objections.

'Now, whether you like it or not, Val, I'm going to finish. You're young, successful, attractive. You dress well. If you made any effort at all, you could probably have any man you wanted. But you have to meet them first. This date with Don is a perfect chance to get back into circulation.' She paused for a moment, biting her lower lip, then heaved a sigh. 'There, that's all I have to say. I'm sorry if you're mad at me for stepping out of line, but I had to do it.'

Val had to smile. 'No, of course I'm not mad at you, Janet. I know you mean well. And I promise I'll think over what you said. You just might have a point.'

That night during her dreary solitary supper, which consisted of a can of chicken gumbo soup eaten out of the pan, two crackers, a glass of milk and a squishy brown banana, Val did think it over. It was pouring outside, and she stood beside the stove in her kitchen listening to the radio slashing in sheets against the window-pane.

It had been a profound shock to come face to face with Michael that day. She had hoped never to see him again, and from his cool, distant manner towards her he had obviously harboured the same sentiments. Behind the icy blue eyes had lain a smouldering resentment, an abiding anger that hadn't diminished since the last time they met. She wished now that she'd followed her impulse and gone back out into the shop to tell him she was sorry she'd ever said he was responsible for what happened to David.

Then, all of a sudden, it hit her. The truth finally sank in. No one was to blame! Not Michael, not his mother, not Myra Barnes, not even Val herself. It was David who had taken that drink, got behind the wheel of the car and smashed it.

A great sense of relief descended on her, like a warm blanket. Here they'd all been, accusing each other, blaming themselves, wrapped in guilt and resentment, when the simple truth was staring them in the face. It was no one's fault!

Furthermore, Janet did have a point. At least, before the episode with Michael, she'd gone out with men when she was asked—even men like Don Carter, who had absolutely nothing to offer her except, as Janet put it, a chance to circulate. What was she going to do—spend the rest of her life in hibernation just because of one bad experience?

On a sudden impulse, and before she could change her mind, she set the pot of soup back down on the stove and marched straight down into her bedroom. She got out her address book from the drawer in the table beside the bed, flipped it open to the 'C's, then picked up the telephone and dialled.

'Hello,' came the lazy voice.

'Don, this is Val Cochran. I just called to tell you that I can make it Saturday night after all. That is, unless you've made other plans.'

'No,' he said quickly. 'No other plans at all. I'm delighted you can go with me. As I said, it'll be boring, but it can't last forever. Maybe we can get away early and do something interesting when it's over. I'll pick you up at your place around seven.'

When they'd hung up, Val glanced at her reflection in the mirror over her dressing-table. She had on an old woollen bathrobe, she was wearing no make-up, and her hair was once again pinned back in the old severe chignon.

'It doesn't look too promising,' she muttered aloud, 'but there's still hope.'

CHAPTER EIGHT

ON SATURDAY afternoon, in a determined effort to improve her deteriorating appearance, Val had her hair done at Seattle's most exclusive—and expensive—salon, putting herself entirely in the hands of the clucking young hairdresser, who circled around her frowning and muttering to himself as he snipped at the ragged ends of her long hair.

'Such a shame,' he said accusingly as he worked. 'To let such beautiful, thick, healthy hair get into such a state.'

Val had to bite her tongue to keep from blurting out an apology at each critical comment. It's my hair, after all, she kept telling herself. Still, he managed to make her feel very guilty about the months of neglect, when all she'd done was wash it every few days, blow it dry and pin it back severely.

After a brisk, invigorating shampoo, the swishy young man set it in large rollers and put her under the drier. When it was done, she sat in the swivel-chair in front of the mirror while he combed it out, still commenting under his breath as he worked.

'Now, that's more like it,' he said with satisfaction when he had finished.

He turned her chair to the mirror and stood behind her, beaming down at her reflection, happy at last. When Val got her first glimpse of the results, a slow, pleased smile spread across her face at what she saw. The transformation in her appearance was truly remarkable. Shorter now, her hair fell in loose waves that turned under at the ends and just covered her ears.

The hairdresser was still looking at her as though she were a work of art he had just created. 'Your hair has such wonderful body,' he gushed as he smoothed it lightly with his hands. 'And see how the right conditioner brings out the lovely blonde highlights and makes it gleam? You should always wear it that way, loose.'

Val's smile faded. That was almost exactly what Michael had said that day they had gone swimming together at Marsh Creek. Although the memory was still vivid in her mind, it seemed like a hundred years ago.

She looked up at the hairdresser. 'Thank you. You've done a wonderful job.'

While she was at it, she decided to have a facial and a manicure. No point in half measures. If she really wanted a new image she might as well go all out.

That night, she made a thorough survey of her wardrobe. It was to be a formal affair, with all of Seattle society in attendance, a good opportunity to wear one of the long dresses hanging in her wardrobe that never got a chance to go anywhere.

She finally settled on a slinky black gown made of silk wool. It had long, fitted sleeves and a very wide, low square neckline that barely covered her shoulders. The neckline set off her long neck, creamy throat and shoulders so nicely that she wouldn't need any jewellery except her grandmother's diamond earrings.

All her pains seemed worth it that night when Don came to get her and she saw the way his eyes lit up the minute she opened the door and he got his first look at her.

'Val, you look sensational,' he said. 'You'll knock 'em dead.'

It was sprinkling lightly outside that night, but since it was only a short walk from Val's condo to Don's car, and at the hotel they parked under the canopy in front to take advantage of the valet parking, they arrived with her new hairstyle in perfect condition.

In the foyer of the hotel, Don checked their coats, and they walked inside the large main ballroom, where Don immediately began to greet his friends, waving and calling to them.

Val glanced around at the crowd gathered in the cavernous room. There was a head table, presumably where the guest of honour and his minions were seated, surrounded by smaller tables for the other guests.

All of a sudden, she felt Don's hand clutch at her arm, his fingers digging into her. Startled, she looked up at him, wondering what had happened. He was grinning broadly, staring straight ahead, his hand raised in greeting.

'Diana!' he called in a loud voice above the noise of the crowd. He turned to Val, his handsome face glowing. 'I just spotted my cousin and her new man. Let's go see if we can find room to sit at their table.'

Before his statement had registered in her fuddled brain, Don had tightened his grasp on her arm and was propelling her across the floor directly towards the front row on the opposite side of the room, where a single couple was seated at a table for four.

The woman was a lovely blonde, and as they came closer Val recognised Diana Worth. Suddenly a horrible suspicion hit her. She stopped short and turned to Don.

'Diana Worth is your cousin?' she asked in a faltering tone.

'Yes. Do you know her?'

'She's one of my customers.'

Don grinned. 'Poor you.'

She hesitated, but when Don kept tugging at her insistently, she knew she had no choice but to follow along. As they came closer, her heart sank with a dull thud. As she had feared, the 'new man' with Diana was Michael Prescott, resplendent in a beautifully tailored dinner-jacket. Their heads were close together, and Diana had one hand resting possessively on his arm.

Don gave her a nudge and bent his head close to hers. 'Be nice to Diana,' he said in a low voice. 'She's Grandfather's favourite. It's disgusting the way the old goat dotes on her, but she wields a lot of clout with him, and I really need that loan.'

Val could only stumble along at his side and pray that the two empty seats at the table were taken. Of all places to run into Michael again! Would she never be free of him?

When they reached the table, Don beamed down at Diana, who merely glanced up at him with a rather mocking little smile on her face, one perfect eyebrow lifted.

'Good evening, Diana,' Don said, bending down to peck her on the cheek. 'You're looking more beautiful than ever. May we join you?'

'Hello, Don,' she drawled. 'What brings you out to the family festivities? You must want something.'

Don laughed shortly. 'Ah, Diana,' he said smoothly. 'You will have your little joke.'

He pulled out one of the chairs for Val, who sat down gingerly, miserable with embarrassment at the awkward situation. Diana's mouth was still curled in a knowing smile, and it was obvious she had little love or respect for her feckless cousin.

Don launched into the introductions. 'Diana, I'd like to have you meet a friend of mine, Val Cochran. Val, this gorgeous creature, believe it or not, is my cousin.'

Diana gave Val a sharp look, as though trying to place her, while Val murmured a brief acknowledgement of the introduction, praying the woman wouldn't recognise her from the boutique. There probably wasn't much danger of that, however, since women like Diana hardly viewed the menials who waited on her as real human beings.

Finally, with a curt 'How do you do?' the blonde nodded at Val.

'Aren't you going to introduce me to your friend?' Don was asking her now. 'Although I believe we may have already met.' He turned to Michael. 'You look quite familiar, at any rate.'

'I don't believe so,' Michael said in a distant voice.

Diana gave an airy wave of her hand. 'Oh, you've probably seen his picture in the newspaper. He's quite a local celebrity.' She gave him a melting smile, then reached across the table and put her hand over his. 'Aren't you, darling?'

'Hardly that,' Michael replied stiffly. He withdrew his hand.

Diana turned back to Don. 'This is Michael Prescott, Don. *Dr* Michael Prescott, the new head of the university cardiac research centre that Grandfather is funding.'

Aha, Val thought, with a sudden little glow. So that's it! If Diana Worth was the granddaughter of the money man behind Michael's new position, that was probably why he was dancing such assiduous attention on her.

But she corrected herself immediately. Diana Worth didn't need that kind of bait to interest a man. Her beauty stood on its own merits. She would be sought after if she were as poor as Val herself. The wealth in her background only made her even more desirable.

While Diana and Don chatted familiarly about family matters, friends and acquaintances, Val sat in stony silence, clutching her evening bag tightly in her lap and staring straight ahead, wishing she were anywhere in the world but at that table with that man sitting next to her.

Michael, on the other hand, seemed relaxed enough. He was lounging comfortably back in his chair, glancing around the room. If the dead silence between them bothered him, he certainly gave no indication of it.

Suddenly Don rose abruptly to his feet. Val jumped visibly, then sat and watched him with dismay as he strode quickly over to Diana's chair and began to pull it out for her. She rose up from it gracefully, languidly.

'Excuse us for a moment, darling,' she said to Michael. 'Don and I really should go speak to Grandfather before the ceremonies get under way.'

Don winked at Val. 'We'll be back shortly.'

Well, at least Don is getting what he wants, Val thought miserably as she watched them walk off together towards the head table. Apparently he had managed to sweet-talk Diana into helping him wangle the money he needed out of their rich grandfather.

In the meantime, what was she supposed to do about Michael now that they were alone? She couldn't even look at him, much less think of anything to say to him.

Just then a white-coated waiter appeared at the table carrying a tray loaded with champagne glasses and dishes of canapés. Val breathed a sigh of relief.

'Would you care for champagne?' the waiter asked.

'Yes, please,' Val said hurriedly, and reached for the glass the moment he set it down before her.

The interruption was short-lived, however, and in just a few seconds they were alone again. But after a few quick swallows of the sparkling wine Val's spirits began to revive. She was sorry she'd come, sorrier she was stuck here alone with the last man on earth she wanted to see, but it was only one evening. Soon the ceremony would begin, and it would all be over.

It occurred to her then in a flash of inspiration that this chance meeting could even be a blessing in disguise. It just might be a perfect opportunity to speak to him, to tell him what she'd come to believe was the truth about David's death. It would probably be the last chance she'd ever have.

She gave him a swift sideways glance. He was gazing off into the distance, his eyes half closed, his jaw set firmly, turning his full champagne glass around on the table-top in slow circles, a habit of his she once found endearing, but which now made her even jumpier than she already was.

Gathering all her courage, she turned to him. 'Michael,' she said in a low voice.

His head came slowly around, and he lifted one heavy dark eyebrow. 'Yes?' he said in a flat, clipped voice.

'Michael, I'm as annoyed as you are at being thrown together like this tonight. I had no idea Diana was Don's cousin, much less that you'd be here with her.'

She paused for a moment, but he only gave her a polite enquiring look and said nothing. Obviously he had no intention of helping her out, and she began to grow irritated at his stubborn silence. But when she saw the little pulse beating along his jawline, she realised that he was not feeling quite as dispassionate as he pretended. She fought down her irritation and plunged ahead.

'However, since this may be the last time we'll ever see each other again, I'd like to apologise for what I said to you about your part in David's death when I left your mother's house that night in Carleton.'

He simply sat and stared at her for several moments. Finally, he cocked his head to one side and gave her a penetrating look, the blue eyes boring into her.

'Just what is it you want from me, Val?' he asked quietly.

'Nothing,' she replied hastily. 'Nothing at all. I just don't want us to be enemies and am only trying to tell you that I'm sorry. It was a rotten thing to say, and I didn't really mean it, but I was very upset at the time——'

She broke off when she saw the colour suffuse his face. His lips were stretched tightly over his teeth, and the pulse at his jaw was pounding furiously as he leaned towards her, menace in every inch of him. She drew back, almost physically afraid of him.

'*You* were upset!' he ground out between half-clenched teeth. 'I explained all I'm going to about that. You chose not to believe me. I don't want to hear anything more on the subject, not ever again.'

Val took a deep breath and forced herself to stay calm. 'I had no intention of rehashing that aspect of it,' she said stiffly. 'I was only trying to explain why I said what I did about blaming you for David's problems.'

'Well, you can forget it. I don't give a damn what you said.' He narrowed his eyes at her and leaned even closer. 'You walked out on me, remember.'

She felt her temper rising out of control. 'You're one to talk!' she snapped angrily. 'Don't think I've forgotten the dirty trick you played, leading me on, making me believe——'

'Hah!' he broke in. 'You know damned good and well that the real reason you went storming out of there without even listening to me wasn't because of anything I said or did, but because of your own stupid paranoia.'

She opened her mouth to protest, but in the next second his eyes glazed over and his face became a mask. He settled back in his chair and shifted his gaze beyond her. She turned around to see that Don and Diana had returned and were standing there staring down at them. Don had a broad pleased grin on his face, but Diana looked livid.

Don sat down next to Val, put an arm around her and gave her a loud smack on the cheek. Her first impulse was to pull away, but when she saw that Michael's eyes were fixed firmly on her, and the sardonic look on his face, she forced herself to sit still. All of a sudden it seemed very important to her to prove to him that she was able to attract and respond to another man.

She turned to Don and gave him her brightest smile. 'You seem to be pretty pleased about something.'

'Oh, I am.'

Just then, out of the corner of her eye, she saw Diana go over to stand behind Michael's chair. She leaned down, her face next to his, and put a hand on his shoulder.

'Come on, darling,' she said in a commanding tone. 'I want Grandfather to meet you.' She gave a brittle laugh. 'After all, since it was largely his money that funded the new cardiac centre, he'll want to get to know its new chief.'

Michael gazed up at her for a few moments with a rather quizzical expression, then slowly rose to his feet. Diana threaded her arm through his, and as they walked off she turned back to Don and Val.

'You will excuse us, won't you?'

'They make a handsome couple, don't they?' Don said as they threaded their way through the crowd.

Val detected a note of sarcasm in his tone and gave him an enquiring look. He was grinning from ear to ear.

'Yes, they do,' she said briefly. 'But what's so funny?'

'Well, for one thing, Diana has had so many men dancing attendance on her that I'm surprised she's settled for one at a time. I just wonder how much that chief's job was worth to him.'

'What do you mean?'

He shrugged. 'Diana has a habit of going full bore after what she wants, then not wanting it quite so much when she gets it.' He put his elbows on the table and leaned towards her. 'But that's not important. What I'm really pleased about is that it looks as though I might get that loan after all. Grandfather is in a mellow mood tonight, with all the fuss and attention everyone is paying him.'

'I'm happy for you, Don.'

'See,' he said. 'I told you you'd bring me luck.' He rose from his chair. 'Now we can get out of here.'

'Aren't you going to stay for the ceremony?'

He lifted his shoulders. 'Why should I? I got what I came for. The rest will only be boring.'

One afternoon a week later, Val and Janet were in the shop getting the Christmas display in order. It was almost leaving time, and they were both tired.

'Why don't you go on home?' Val said at last. 'I'm going to stay another hour or two and try to finish up at least this one window, but there's no point in both of us wearing ourselves out.'

'I don't mind staying,' Janet replied. 'In fact, we could both stay and just get it over with.'

'Aren't you starved? I know I am.'

'Why don't you go out and get a bite to eat, then? I'll go when you come back.'

'Well, if you're sure.' The little bell at the top of the front door jangled just then. 'I'll go,' Val said. 'You finish up here. When I'm through with this customer I'll go right on and get some dinner.'

When she walked out into the front of the shop, her heart lurched sickeningly when she saw Michael standing just inside the door. Her steps slowed and she stopped about five feet away from him, staring. He was wearing a tan trench coat over a dark suit, raindrops sparkled in his black hair, and he looked wonderful.

'Hello, Val,' he said quietly. 'I thought it might be about quitting time and I wanted to catch you before you left.'

'What do you want, Michael?'

He shrugged and took a step towards her. 'Just to talk to you. Can we have a drink somewhere? Or dinner, if you like? I could drive you home. It's pouring outside.'

'No, thanks. I'm not going right home.'

He raised an eyebrow and smiled. 'Got a date?'

'No. I have to work.' She could have bitten her tongue out. What had made her blurt out the truth like that?

'Well, you have to eat,' he persisted. 'Surely you can bear with my company for an hour or so? And I really would like to speak to you.'

Val debated. What could it hurt? A quick drink and a sandwich and then it would be over. She couldn't imagine what in the world he had to say to her after their last stormy encounter, but he'd roused her curiosity.

'All right,' she said at last. 'I'll just tell Janet I'm leaving.' She hurriedly retraced her steps and stood just outside the door to the workroom. 'I'm going now, Janet,' she called.

Janet looked up. 'What happened to the customer?'

Val made a wry face. 'That's who I'm leaving with.'

Before Janet had a chance to ask any more questions, Val turned quickly and went back out into the shop. Michael opened the front door for her, and as they walked out into the wide corridor Val glanced back and saw Janet staring after them, goggle-eyed.

'There's a decent little restaurant down on the main floor,' Val said briskly as they walked towards the staircase. 'I was going out to have a bite to eat anyway, and that's as good a place as any.'

The Blue Goose was popular with the downtown business people, but did most of its business during the lunch hour. Now, at six o'clock on a rainy Friday afternoon, it was virtually empty. They were ushered right away into one of the vacant booths in the dining-room by a waitress, who stood there pad in hand while they seated themselves across from each other.

'Would you like a drink first?' Michael asked.

'No. I don't think so. It'll only make me sleepy and I still have a lot of work to do tonight.'

Michael looked at the waitress. 'Nothing to drink, thanks,' he said. 'We'll take a few minutes with the menu.'

When she was gone, Michael turned back to Val and gazed across at her for several moments. He seemed to be trying to make up his mind how to begin. She wasn't going to help him out. He'd asked for the meeting. It was up to him to carry the ball.

She glanced hastily over the menu. She'd lost what appetite she'd had. In a few moments the waitress came back. Val set her menu down and looked up at her.

'I'll just have coffee,' she said.

Michael handed his menu to the waitress. 'I think I'll have that drink after all,' he said. 'A Scotch and soda, please.' He turned to Val. 'Are you sure you're not hungry?'

'Not just yet,' she said.

There was another long silence until the waitress returned with their order. When she was gone, Michael took a long swallow of his drink, then lit a cigarette, while Val watched him covertly, wondering what in the world it was he had on his mind that he would make a special trip into town on such a nasty evening just to seek her out.

The maddening thing was that she still found him so appealing. The way his hands moved as he lit the match, shook it out and dropped it in the ashtray, the concentrated expression on his lean face, and when his eyes fastened on her, too late for her to look away, they still had the power to hold her in their steady blue gaze.

He braced his elbows on the table and leaned forwards, frowning down at his drink and moving it around in slow circles, obviously hesitant to begin.

Val steeled herself against him. He'd tricked her once when she'd trusted him. She wasn't going to make that mistake again. Even though she did hope for an end to hostilities between them, to wipe the slate clean, she couldn't forget the hurt she'd felt when she'd found out he was only using her.

Finally he settled back and raised his head. 'I've been thinking over what you said last Saturday night at that dreadful reception.' He smiled faintly and took a sip of his drink. 'Although I gather it turned out quite well for your Don Carter.'

Val was just about to tell him that he wasn't *her* Don Carter, but clamped her jaw shut just in time. Let him think what he liked. She raised her cup to her lips and took a quick swallow of coffee.

'At any rate,' he went on, 'I just wanted to let you know that I think you were right, that harbouring grudges about a past that can't be altered in any way only does harm, for all concerned. And so, I'd like to say categorically, in plain English, once and for all, that I know you were in no way to blame for David's death and that I was dead wrong to concoct that silly scheme to pay you back for what I thought you did to him.'

Val eyed him suspiciously. Was he sincere? Finally she nodded. 'I'm very glad to hear that. If you really mean it.'

'Oh, I mean it, all right,' he said with feeling. 'As a matter of fact, I had a little talk with Myra Barnes before I left Carleton. She told me what had really happened that night, that she'd encouraged David to take that first drink, and then it got out of hand. It was too late to stop him.'

'I hope you haven't made any plans to get revenge on her, too,' Val commented drily.

When she saw the deep red colour wash from his neck up over his face, she immediately regretted her words. He jabbed his cigarette out viciously in the ashtray, lifted his head and drained the rest of his drink in one long swallow.

'I'm sorry,' Val murmured. 'That was low.'

He nodded shortly. 'I probably had it coming. No, I don't blame Myra, and I've already told her so.' He shrugged. 'As a matter of fact, I knew the truth long before Myra confirmed it. That's what I wanted to talk to you about. You were right. No one is to blame. It was one of those tragedies that just happen. None of us caused it, and none of us could have prevented it, yet all of us felt guilty, including me. You were right about that, too. I probably could have done a lot more to help David after our father died, taken more of an interest in him and his problems, but I was too busy with my career.'

She fixed him with a steady gaze. 'I didn't mean it. I shouldn't have said it. Like you, I felt guilty—and angry at the trick you'd played on me—so I lashed out at you. I'm sorry.'

'It wasn't a trick, Val,' he said in a low, earnest voice. 'You've got to believe me.' He waved a hand in the air. 'Oh, I admit it started out that way. I was half out of my mind for a few days after the accident. Seeing you at the funeral, then at my mother's place—you were the only target in sight for my helpless rage. I felt I had to *do* something. I knew how much you meant to David, how crushed he was when you left. Seeing that you'd come back, I put two and two together and got five.'

'I can understand how you would,' she said. 'I can't even blame you. But did you have to carry it quite so far?' Her cheeks burned at the memory of that last afternoon.

'By then,' he said quietly, 'the game was over. What happened between us had no part in it. I hope you'll believe that.'

Val searched his face carefully. He seemed sincere. He was obviously waiting for some sign from her, a word, a gesture. But could she trust him? What was it he really wanted from her? A little flicker of hope began to move deep inside her. Could they possibly start over again, this time on a more realistic and open basis?

Much as she tried to deny it, she'd been in love with this man once, so much so that she'd gone to bed with him. While that seemed to be no big deal in today's liberated sexual climate, to Val it had been a momentous step. If she let herself, she knew that even now he had the power to make her fall in love with him again.

'Yes,' she said at last. 'I believe you.'

'Good,' he said with patent relief. 'It's weighed terribly on my mind.' He glanced at her empty cup. 'Would you like a refill? Or a bite to eat?'

'No, thanks.'

He slid over across the booth and got up to stand beside the table, looking down at her. 'Then shall we go? I know you're anxious to get back to your shop. This must be a busy season for you.'

If he'd thrown a glass of cold water in her face, Val couldn't have been more stunned. Was that all there was to it? Surely not. Slowly she got out of the booth and walked with him to the register in the lobby.

After he'd paid the bill, they went out on to the main floor, crowded now with the early evening Christmas shoppers milling about. At the foot of the stairs, he stopped and turned to her.

'I'll leave you now,' he said. 'I'm glad we've had this little talk. It's a great relief to me to have the slate wiped clean. I feel much better about it, and I hope you do, too.'

He reached for her hand, shook it briefly, then, with a slight dip of his dark head, turned and walked away from her towards the entrance, shrugging on his trench coat as he went.

Val stood there gawking at his retreating tall figure for several long seconds, her hand still foolishly outstretched, until finally he disappeared through the revolving doors.

She dropped her hand, then turned and started walking slowly up the stairs. She could hardly believe what had just happened and was still in a mild state of shock. She'd been so certain this overture of his would be a new beginning for them. Was it just another trick?

Of course not. He just wasn't interested in her. Why should he be when he had the beautiful—and *rich*—Diana Worth to play with? There wasn't much to choose between there.

By the time she battled her way through thc hordes of shoppers every step of the way and reached the top of the stairs, she had to admit that it was probably better to end it this way. There was too much bitter history between them for anything else. They could never be friends, but at least they were no longer enemies.

When she went inside the shop, Janet was just coming from the back room with an armload of decorations for the small Christmas tree they had set up in the front window. When she saw Val, she stopped short and goggled at her.

'That was quick.' She grinned and came up to her. 'I thought you might be gone for good. Where's Mr Wonderful?'

'He had to leave.'

'Well?'

Val sighed. 'Well, what?'

'What happened?'

'Nothing happened,' Val replied casually. 'We had some old unfinished family business to take care of, that's all.'

Janet's face fell. 'Oh. I'm sorry.'

So am I, Val thought as she breezed past her. So am I.

CHAPTER NINE

CHRISTMAS came and went in a blur of frantic activity at the shop, always their busiest season. This suited Val. As she had spent every Christmas alone since her grandmother died, to her it was just another day anyway. This year she was especially grateful for the many long hours she had to spend working. It helped keep her mind off that last dreary meeting with Michael.

He had been so smug, so well pleased with himself, had actually acted as though he were doing her a favour with his magnanimous offer of a truce, an end to hostilities between them. But then, he had the lovely Diana to turn to. Diana, with her arrogant self-assurance, her wealth, position, connections. He could well afford to be gracious with a woman like that for support.

In the meantime, Val had a business to run, with little time to brood about her personal life. Soon it would be January, a brand new year, and time for one of their two big annual sales. Then, in February, the yearly inventory.

'There's no reason why you can't take a few days off to go visit your family in Spokane if you want to,' she said to Janet a few days after Christmas. 'After all, you didn't get to spend the holidays with them.'

Janet shot her a dubious look. 'Are you sure?'

Val nodded. 'There's always a lull about this time before the big January sale. Except for exchanges, we won't have much business until next week.'

'Well, thanks, Val,' Janet said. 'I think I'll just take you up on that.' There was a short silence as she finished marking the blouses on the work table. Then she asked casually, 'What about you? Any exciting plans for New Year's Eve?'

'Oh, not really,' Val replied. 'I guess I'll just go to the bash at the yacht club with Don Carter.'

Janet goggled at her. '*Just* the bash at the yacht club? I'd say that's travelling in pretty exalted circles.'

Val shrugged. 'I guess.'

'So, how are things going? I mean you and Don. He seems like a nice guy. Attractive. Good family.'

'I suppose so.' Val smiled. 'But we're just good friends. It's hard to take Don seriously. He's such a clown. He just coasts through life on the strength of his charm and family connections.'

'Doesn't sound as though you consider him very promising husband material,' Janet mused thoughtfully.

Val laughed out loud. 'Don? You're joking. He's amusing and makes a decent escort, when he's sober, but that's about it.'

It was raining on New Year's Eve, one of those cold, sleety downpours that hovered on the edge of snow but never quite made it. Don dropped her off at the entrance to the club to go and park the car, and Val stood on the steps, shivering in her heavy black coat, waiting for him, listening to the music and the noise of the crowd inside.

Half-heartedly getting ready for the party earlier that evening, Val would have done anything to get out of going, even to the point of manufacturing possible excuses. Don wouldn't really have cared. There were always plenty of unattached women in his crowd who would be glad of an extra man.

In the end, however, she hadn't quite been able to bring herself to do it. If she stayed home she'd only start brooding again. Besides, she'd bought a new dress, a brilliantly patterned long silk wool that draped beautifully on her too thin figure. It was cut high at the neckline, to hide the sharp collarbones, then tapered gradually into a deep V in the back. The vibrant colours—red, green, blue and yellow Paisley on a black background—were chosen deliberately to lift her spirits and put her in a party mood.

Finally, Don came loping down the steep pavement that led to the entrance of the yacht club, his overcoat collar turned up, his face red from the cold. He put his arm around her and led her inside where it was warm.

'What a rotten, God-forsaken climate we live in,' he said, stamping his feet and chafing his cold hands. 'Come on.'

They took off their coats and checked them at the door, then made their way into the main room. Except for the different location and festive decorations, it was an exact replica of the reception he'd taken her to in his grandfather's honour. The same faces, the same exclusive little groups at the tables, the same loud chatter. The small orchestra was even playing the same music.

Don led her to a table for eight right on the dance-floor, and as he seated her Val breathed an inner sigh of relief to see that Michael and Diana were not among the other six people present. With luck, they wouldn't show up at all, and she put on her most pleasant social smile as Don introduced her to his friends, determined to have a good time if it killed her.

By midnight, however, she'd had enough of trying to pretend she was having a good time, sick of grinning at this roomful of strangers, and Don most of all. If she'd had any idea what he'd had in mind when he'd said he wanted to celebrate, she never would have come in the first place.

He'd spent most of the evening flitting around from table to table, paying court to his influential friends and gloating over the good news of the loan he'd wangled from his grandfather. On the rare occasions when he did come to light in the chair next to Val, it was only to down one potent Scotch after another.

Val's facial muscles were rigid from the fixed smile she'd struggled to maintain throughout the whole boring evening, and when at last the New Year was ushered in with the traditional singing of 'Auld Lang Syne', the streamers and confetti littering everything in sight and the obligatory slobbering midnight kiss, her one thought was to go home, with or without Don Carter.

Standing in the middle of the crowded dance-floor, she told him so, as pleasantly as she could, the false grin still in place.

'Oh, come on, Val,' he protested loudly, slurring his words. 'Don't be a wet blanket. The evening is young.'

'I'm sorry, Don,' she countered lightly but firmly. 'But I'm really tired.' Before he could start to argue with her again, she added, 'Listen, I can find my own way home. I'll just call a cab. There's no reason for you to miss out on the rest of the party.'

'No,' he said with determination. 'I won't hear of it. I brought you. I'll take you home.'

Val wondered just how drunk he was. She didn't live far away. At least they wouldn't have to get out on the treacherous interstate, and, given the usual heavy New Year's Eve traffic on the side-streets, he'd have to drive at a snail's pace anyway.

She made one more effort to object, but Don was so insistent that she decided to humour him just so he wouldn't create a scene. It would probably be all right.

It was still raining outside, and the streets were slick, but, like many drunks, Don drove with extra caution. Still, Val breathed a sigh of relief when they reached the intersection at the bottom of Queen Anne Hill. Just a few more minutes, and they'd be at her place. She really should try to get some coffee down him before he left.

When the traffic light turned green, Don crept out into the intersection to make his right turn up the steep hill. Suddenly out of nowhere, another car came hurtling towards them, speeding fast, its headlights glaring at them through the rain-spattered windscreen.

The last thing Val was conscious of before the oncoming car swerved to make a left turn directly in their path was that blinding glare, then a sickening crunch, then total blackness.

She fought her way towards consciousness with a splitting headache and a feeling of total disorientation. She had no idea where she was or how she got there or what had happened. The only reality was the awful pounding pain.

Cautiously, she opened one eye, then shut it quickly as a blinding glare sent a fresh stab of the knife into her head. Dimly she heard someone call her name, a low voice, barely audible, as though coming across a great distance.

'Val. Val, are you awake?'

She tried to nod, but that only made the pain worse. She lay perfectly still, her eyes shut tight, and tried to blot out all consciousness. Wherever she was, how she got there, didn't matter. The mere effort of thinking about it made her head spin.

She felt a slight pinprick of pain in her arm, nothing compared to the twisting agony behind her eyes, then, in a few moments, blessedly, gratefully, she drifted into the void.

When she came to the second time, the pain wasn't quite so devastating as before, and when her eyes fluttered open the brilliant glare seemed to be gone, or at least diminished.

Slowly, gingerly, she shifted her gaze to glance around at her surroundings. She was in a small room, white everywhere, the walls, the curtains at the window, the bed she was lying on. There was a faint medicinal tang in the air, and the sound of footsteps and muffled voices came from beyond the half-open door.

She had a vague recollection now of being in a car at night, a slick street, oncoming headlights, a loud crunching noise, then—the rest was a blank. She must have been in an automobile accident, and obviously was now in the hospital.

She closed her eyes and concentrated on trying to recall the details of the accident, but her mind couldn't seem to function beyond one clear fact: she was certain she had not been driving. She wondered how badly she was hurt. The only real distress she was experiencing was inside her head, which still throbbed dully.

Just to make sure, she began cautiously to test the responses in the rest of her body, wiggling her toes, flexing the muscles of her legs and arms, moving her fingers feebly. Although there were a few minor twinges elsewhere, everything seemed to be in decent working order.

She slept again, and the next time she woke up she distinctly heard the patter of rain against the window. She smiled to herself. That could only mean she was still in Seattle.

When she opened her eyes, they fell immediately on a dark shape at the foot of the bed. She struggled painfully to focus on it, and gradually became aware that it was the figure of a man standing there, white-coated, obviously a doctor. He was holding a clip-board with a metal backing, frowning down at it in deep concentration.

She recognised him the moment her eyes became accustomed to the dim light. It was Michael! A deep feeling of relief and joy surged through her. Michael would take care of her. She tried to raise her head and call his name, but even the slightest movement set up a shower of blinding sparks in her head. She clenched her jaw in agony, and all that came out was a weak croak.

Instantly, at the sound, his head came up and he moved swiftly to the side of the bed. He reached down and put his fingers on her wrist, held them there for several seconds, then leaned over her.

'Val. Val, can you hear me?'

She gazed up at him and managed a weak smile. 'Michael? Yes, I can hear you.'

'Do you remember what happened? Do you know where you are?'

'Vaguely. I know I've been in an automobile accident, and I'm fairly certain I wasn't driving, but I can't recall any of the details.'

He nodded. 'It'll all come back in time. For now all you need to know is that you're at the university hospital. You have a concussion and a few bruises, but no serious injuries.' His voice was low and gentle, but quite clear. He spoke slowly, in deliberate measured tones, as though to make certain she understood.

'A concussion?' she asked in a small voice.

Suddenly frightened, she groped for his hand, and immediately felt the large, strong warmth of it as it closed over hers, pressing gently, reassuringly.

'It's not a severe one,' he said quickly. 'Since you regained consciousness within twenty-four hours, you should have a complete recovery. But even a moderate concussion isn't a pleasant experience. Are you in much pain?'

'No. Not now. Not as bad as it was, anyway.'

'Do you want me to give you something for it? Actually, it's better if you're not sedated.'

'No. I can manage.'

'It'll pass gradually. In a few days you'll be as good as new.'

She was growing groggy again, but she had an insistent nagging feeling at the back of her mind that there was a cloudy issue between them that had to be resolved before she could relax and go to sleep again. Her memory was still hazy, and, although she felt deeply that she loved this man and he loved her, she had to know for sure. She looked into the beautiful blue eyes, bright and clear even in the dim room, and managed another smile.

'Michael,' she said thickly, 'everything *is* all right, isn't it?'

'Of course,' he said. 'I told you. You'll be fine in a day or two.' He started to pull his hand away from hers. 'I'll leave you now. You need your rest.'

Alarmed, she clutched frantically at his hand and gazed up at him in panic. 'No. That isn't what I meant. I mean, between us. There's nothing wrong, is there, darling? You know how much I love you.'

The blue eyes narrowed in a puzzled look, and he jerked his head back sharply with a swift hushed intake of breath. 'Val . . .' he began in a low worried tone.

'Please,' she begged. 'Just hold me for a while.'

After a moment's hesitation, he smiled, bent down, and she felt his arms come around her, the scrape of his cheek against hers, the clean, slightly medicinal scent of his crisp white coat filling her nostrils, his lips brushing lightly on hers. Her eyes closed and she began to drift off, safe in his arms.

After a few moments she felt him raise up. He sat quite still for a moment, smoothing her hair back from her forehead, then eased himself off the side of the bed.

'Go to sleep now,' he said softly. 'I'll look in on you a little later and we can talk more then.'

She nodded happily. He gave her hand one last gentle squeeze, then laid it down carefully, turned and walked quietly out of the room.

When he was gone, Val lay there wakeful for a while, filled with the warmth and well-being his presence always brought her. Michael! He made her feel so safe, so secure. She loved him so much, and now she was satisfied that he loved her, too. The way he'd held her hand, the tender look on his face, the kiss, all reassured her of that.

But, wait a minute. Her eyes flew open and she frowned as the nagging little worry reasserted itself. There was more to it than that, something she'd forgotten. It had to do with the puzzled, almost startled look on his face when she'd told him she loved him. Something bad, something painful she didn't want to remember. But she must! What could it be?

She searched her mind, but all she could come up with was a vision of the two of them, she and Michael, two people in love. They *were* lovers—or had been—she was certain of that. Even in her drugged, semiconscious state, she was absolutely positive that she knew every inch of his body intimately, understood his mind, the kind of person he was. That was all that mattered.

Satisfied, she closed her eyes. Besides, if there was more, it would come back to her in time.

She was dreaming that Michael had come to her, was holding her, kissing her, when she became dimly aware of sounds and movement in the room, brisk footsteps, the swish of curtains being drawn open, the clank of crockery and silverware, then someone calling to her.

As she struggled to a semi-conscious state, her first thought was to wonder why in the world she should be having erotic dreams about Michael Prescott, a man who had walked out of her life for good. It was almost funny.

Dismissing the dream as an irrelevant drug-induced fantasy, she squinted her eyes narrowly at the bright glare of sunshine coming in through the window. Memory returned immediately this time. She was in the hospital. She had a concussion. Her head still ached, but the dreadful hammering seemed to have lessened considerably.

She smelled food, coffee, and realised she was very hungry. She blinked and opened her eyes all the way to see a short, heavy set woman dressed in a crisp white uniform standing beside her bed and shaking down a thermometer. There was a black badge pinned to her ample bosom: 'P. Jacobs, RN.'

'Good morning, Miss Cochran,' she said cheerily. 'How are we feeling this morning?'

Before Val could answer, P. Jacobs had stuck the thermometer in her mouth and taken hold of her wrist. After a few moments, she retrieved the thermometer, held it up to the light, then went to the foot of the bed to make an entry in the chart.

'All signals normal,' she called. 'You're making fine progress. I'll help you to the bathroom, then we'll have our breakfast. Hungry?'

Val smiled. 'Yes. I'm starved.'

'Good. Head feel any better?'

'Much.'

'Well, then, let's get to work. You can wash, brush your teeth and put on a clean gown, but no shower until later this morning when I have time to help you.'

Even those meagre ablutions went a long way to improving Val's morale, and when she was back in bed, the covers smoothed, the pillows propped up under her head, Nurse Jacobs brought in her breakfast tray and set it down before her.

'Not too appetising, I'm afraid,' she said, lifting the lid off a bowl of greyish gruel, 'but nourishing. You tuck in, and I'll be back in a while for your tray. Don't get out of bed on your own just yet.'

'Don't worry,' Val replied with feeling. The short trip to the bathroom, even with the nurse to support her, had taken all her strength, and she still felt dizzy. 'I'm not about to make any solo flights for a while.'

On her way out of the room, Nurse Jacobs stopped to make one more entry on the chart. Just as she was about to close the metal cover, she pursed her lips and gave Val a sharp disapproving look.

'Well,' she said, 'it seems as though Dr Prescott has been to see you. Wonder what a cardiologist is doing consulting on a simple concussion?' She rolled her eyes heavenwards with a sigh and snapped the chart back in place. 'Doctors!' she commented drily, and strode briskly out of the room.

Val stared after her, her glass of orange juice halfway to her mouth, stunned, as the words sank in. Slowly, the memory of Michael's visit seeped into her mind. It hadn't been a dream! He really *had* been there!

She set the glass down carefully on the tray, rested her head back on the pillows and squeezed her eyes shut tight. As the full details of that last encounter flooded back, she groaned aloud with sheer dismay.

'Oh, no,' she muttered through clenched teeth. Had she really called him darling? Begged him to stay with her? To hold her? Told him she loved him? Assumed he loved her? What had possessed her? At the time she had been absolutely convinced that they *were* lovers.

How could she have done such a thing? An icy chill gripped her. What was far worse, how could she ever face him again? It was too humiliating. To have been all through one rejection, one seduction and betrayal, only to leave herself wide open for yet another one just when she'd closed that chapter of her life for good!

Could she refuse to see him? Maybe he wouldn't come back. Her cheeks burned hotly. What must he think? Surely he must be as embarrassed by that maudlin display as she was. Yet, he was a doctor, after all, and probably used to the ravings of half-conscious patients.

All she could do was hope he didn't return, or that she'd be well enough to leave the hospital first. As a last resort, if he did come back to make another courtesy call, she'd simply act as though nothing at all out of the way had happened between them.

After breakfast, Val slept fitfully most of the morning. The regular doctor in charge of her case came to check her over and pronounced her nicely on the mend, but when she asked him when she could go home he gave her a dubious look.

'Not for another day or two at the minimum,' he said in a typical officious tone. 'We need to keep an eye on concussions for at least three days.'

'But I'm feeling so much better,' she protested.

He shook his head firmly. 'I can't allow it.' And that, obviously, was his final word, since he turned on his heel and walked out of the room before she could argue with him.

Nurse Jacobs came in before lunch to help her shower and wash her hair. It wasn't until after she was back in the freshly made bed, her hair washed and dried, that she suddenly thought about Don. She called to the nurse just as she was leaving.

'Nurse Jacobs, Don Carter, the man who was driving the car the night of the accident. How is he?'

'Oh, he's fine. Just a few minor cuts and bruises. In fact, he's been haunting the nurses' station asking when he'd be able to visit you.'

'I don't really feel up to visitors at the moment,' Val murmured. She had no wish to listen to Don Carter's apologies and self-justifications.

Nurse Jacobs pursed her lips censoriously. 'I suppose you know he was quite intoxicated the night of the accident and should never have been behind the wheel of a car. People in that condition often seem to escape serious injury. It's their poor passengers and the other innocent victims who suffer the consequences.'

With that, she turned and marched out of the room, leaving Val with the feeling that it was somehow all her fault, just because she'd been in the car with Don that night. It probably had been foolish, but actually the accident hadn't really been Don's fault. He'd driven with extreme caution.

Her lunch was slightly more appetising than her breakfast had been, and by mid-afternoon, fed and bathed, her headache almost gone, she began to feel restless. She really should talk to Janet and find out how she was managing all alone at the shop.

There was a telephone on the table beside her bed, but it had been unplugged so she wouldn't be disturbed. A little guiltily, she slipped out of bed, braced herself against the table until the wave of dizziness passed, then plugged the cord into the wall outlet.

She jumped quickly back into bed before a nurse or doctor came in to catch her in the act, then dialled the shop's number.

'Seattle Boutique,' came Janet's voice. 'May I help you?'

'Janet, it's Val. How are you doing?'

'Oh, I'm OK. But how are you? Gosh, it's good to hear your voice. I wanted to come to see you, but they said you couldn't have visitors when I called. How are you feeling?'

'I'm on the mend, thanks. It was only a concussion.'

'*Only* a concussion!'

'Well, nothing serious. I should be out of here in a few days and hope to get back to work right away, at least before the sale starts next week. Tell me, how did you know I was in the hospital?'

'Your friend Don Carter called to let me know.'

'That was nice of him.'

'Nice!' Janet exclaimed. 'He's the one who put you there.'

'It wasn't really his fault. Anyway, are you sure you can handle things at the shop until I get back? We could always try to get you some temporary help.'

'No, I can manage. It's the usual post-holiday lull, and I spend most of my time marking things down for the sale. Listen, do you have a way home from the hospital? I can't leave while the shop's open, but I'd be glad to come and pick you up during my lunch hour.'

'Thanks, Janet. That would be great.'

They discussed the preparations for the sale for a few more minutes, and after Val hung up she stared blankly out of the window as a sudden wave of depression swept over her. It was a sad commentary on her life that the only person she knew in the whole world who would even bother to offer to take her home from the hospital was Janet.

In spite of herself and all her resolutions, her mind wandered to thoughts of Michael. She was still horribly embarrassed at the display she must have put on for him in her half-comatose state. Thankfully he hadn't come again. She'd been half expecting him every time the door opened, dreading it and hoping for it at the same time, and finally had convinced herself he was taking the wisest, most sensible course in ignoring the whole thing.

Just then there was a light rapping on the half-open door, and she looked up to see Don Carter's blond head poking around it. She almost had to laugh out loud at the hangdog expression on his face.

'Can I come in?' he asked in a hushed tone.

Somehow, just seeing him with that ridiculous look, his mouth open, his eyes staring, made her forget her blue mood, and she decided to have a little fun with him.

She raised her arm to cover her forehead and groaned pitiably. For a second it looked as though he was going to turn around and bolt out of the room. He seemed downright terrified. Val took pity on him and, laughing, lowered her arm.

'Come on in, Don,' she called to him. 'I'm only teasing you. I'm fine.'

He tiptoed gingerly over to the side of the bed and stood there looking down at her dubiously. 'Are you sure?' he whispered.

'Yes, I'm sure. Sit down.' She motioned to a chair. 'I was glad to hear that you suffered no ill effects from our little adventure,' she remarked drily.

He perched on the edge of the chair and gave her a tragic look. 'God, Val, I'm so sorry for what happened. How could I have been such a jerk? I've been out of my mind with worry about you.'

'Well, yes,' she agreed with a smile. 'You were a little bit of a jerk, but you can quit worrying. I'm feeling better all the time. In fact, I should get out of here in a day or two.'

'Well, that's a relief!' He expelled a long sigh and settled back in the chair.

Nurse Jacobs came bustling in just then with a vase full of long-stemmed red roses. She shot Don an accusing look, snorting under her breath, and set the flowers down on the dresser.

'From you?' Val asked him.

He nodded. 'It's not much, but if there's anything else I can do——'

'You'll have to leave now, Mr Carter,' the nurse broke in. 'Dr Costello is due any minute on his afternoon rounds.'

Don jumped hastily to his feet, and this time Nurse Jacobs's snort was audible. Don gave her a guilty look, then walked swiftly over to the door. He raised his hand and waved, then was gone.

Late that night, lying wakeful in bed, with only the dim night light burning, the muffled hospital sounds coming from the corridor outside her room, depression descended on Val once again. Only this time there was nothing to distract her from her gloomy thoughts.

No matter how hard she fought them down, the images that kept popping into her mind were all visions of Michael. Finally she had to admit to herself that, as embarrassing as it would have been for both of them to see each other again, she was actually bitterly disappointed that he hadn't come back, as he'd said he would.

She knew it was better that he hadn't. Not only would it have been awkward, but there was no future in it. He would go his way with the lovely Diana Worth, and she would go hers. Alone. She was grateful to Don for his concern, but the idea of any kind of serious relationship with him was only laughable.

She had managed her life by herself before Michael had come bursting into it with his practised seduction, his cruel scheme for revenge, and she could do it again. With this firm intention in mind, she began to feel a little better, and had just started to drift off when the door to her room opened.

She looked up. There, his silhouette outlined by the light from the hallway, stood Michael himself.

CHAPTER TEN

'VAL,' she heard Michael call softly. 'Are you awake?'

She could pretend she was asleep, but what would that gain her? Since he actually had shown up, he'd probably try again. She'd have to face him sooner or later, and might as well get it over with now.

She pushed the pillows up behind her head. 'Yes. I'm awake.'

He came inside, leaving the door open so that the dim room was cast in a wide swath of half-light from the corridor. Val steeled herself as he approached, her hands and feet icy cold, her cheeks burning, praying he wouldn't mention their last encounter. She'd made such a fool of herself!

He stood beside the bed looking down at her, his hands hanging loosely at his sides. Tonight he was dressed in a dark suit and tie. Without the white coat he looked less impersonal, more familiar, and somehow more forbidding. His back was to the light, so she couldn't make out his expression, but when he spoke his voice was normal, the tone bland, even professional.

'I would have come sooner,' he said, 'but I was tied up in meetings all day. How are you feeling?'

'Much better, thank you,' she said stiffly.

'Headache all gone?'

'Yes.'

He sat down on the chair beside the bed and leaned towards her. At closer quarters, she could just make out the smile on his face, the warmth in his gaze. The tears welled up behind her eyes, and she bit her lip to keep them from spilling over. Oh, why did he have to come back? she agonised.

He reached out a hand and placed it on her face, warm and soft, then bent over to kiss her lightly on the cheek. She flinched at his touch and turned her head away. Slowly, she felt the hand being removed. There was utter silence in the room.

'Val,' he said at last, 'what is it?'

Summoning every ounce of her strength, she forced out a smile and turned to face him again. 'Nothing. Just another twinge, that's all.'

There was another awkward silence. Val couldn't think of one sensible thing to say. She couldn't bring up the subject uppermost in her mind, since her hope was to avoid it altogether. But neither could she just make small talk in her current agitated state.

Finally, she seized on the weather as a safe topic. 'Is it still raining——?'

At the same moment, he said, 'Val, about what happened——'

They both broke off simultaneously. It was almost funny, and she had to suppress a wild urge to burst into a hysterical fit of giggles. Well, he'd brought it up. It was in the open now.

She gave a harsh little laugh. 'You know, I have a vague recollection that I said some pretty stupid things to you the last time you were here. If so, I apologise.'

He was silent for a moment, as though absorbing her statement. 'Stupid?' he asked quizzically at last. 'What do you mean?'

Maybe he *had* forgotten! Relief washed over her. Was she really going to be let off that easily? She raised her head up on the pillows a little further and smiled at him.

'Well, if you don't know, then let's just drop it.'

'Just like that?' he asked in a steely tone. 'And what about the things you said, the way you acted?'

She stared at him, dismayed. He was leaning back in the chair, one arm hooked over the back of it, and seemed relaxed enough, but the firm jaw was set, the eyes narrowed angrily at her. Oh, God, she thought, now what do I do? And what did *he* have to be angry about? She was the one who had everything to lose. There was only one hope, to treat the whole thing as a joke.

She waved a dismissive hand in the air. 'Oh, that,' she said lightly. 'Surely with all your medical experience you know enough by now not to take the ravings of a concussed patient seriously.'

He looked at her as though she had struck him. 'That's what it was?' he asked in a tight voice. 'Ravings?'

'Of course,' she replied with a little laugh. 'I'm sorry. It must have been horribly embarrassing for you. I can hardly believe I did such a thing. In fact, I was hoping it was all only a bad dream. Please, let's just forget it.'

He rose to his feet and stood looking down at her, a long, cool gaze, his eyes hooded, his face like thunder. He folded his arms across his chest, and even in the shadows there was no mistaking the look of cold contempt on his face.

'All right,' he said. 'Have it your way.'

He turned on his heel then and stalked away from her. Val stared at his retreating back, the tears smarting once again. What did he want from her?

Why was he putting her through this torture? Was it simply for more revenge? Hadn't he had enough?

At the door, he hesitated for a moment, then turned around. 'I'll leave you with a thought to chew on,' he said distantly. 'On some level you meant what you said, and your actions were a genuine expression of your true feelings, probably for the first time in your life. And you're only lying to yourself—once again—if you pretend differently. Don't ever forget, Val, that it was your paranoia, your fear of trusting, that wrecked our whole relationship in the first place.'

She sat bolt upright in bed. 'No!' she cried, eyes blazing. Her tears were forgotten in a sudden uprush of righteous indignation. How dared he accuse her of destroying their relationship? She raised her arm and pointed an accusing finger at him. 'What wrecked everything was your own pig-headed arrogance, your vindictive scheme to pay me back for hurting David.'

He came part way back inside and stood there between the bed and the door, his long legs apart, his knuckles resting on his hips. 'I explained all that,' he said coldly. 'I was wrong. I admitted it. OK, I did want to see you hurt, the way I thought you'd hurt David. But, damn it, I ended up by falling in love with you.'

Val was utterly speechless. Was this another hallucination? Surely she'd heard him wrong. Her head spun around crazily. Michael was still talking, and she had to make a supreme effort to follow what he was saying.

'It's that damned playboy, Don Carter, isn't it?' he accused in a sneering tone. 'I've seen him hovering around outside your door. For God's sake, Val, I thought you had better taste than that.'

She finally found her tongue. 'Like you, I suppose,' she retorted. 'And how about Diana Worth? I suppose you'd call her a model of womanly virtues.'

'There's no reasoning with you,' he said disgustedly. 'Keep shoring up that wall you've built around yourself, stay in your safe little world.'

If she'd had a heavy object ready at hand, she would have thrown it at him. As it was, all she could do was sit there spluttering with rage, unable to think of one thing nasty enough to hurl after him as a parting word.

Then, suddenly, he was gone, out the door, out of her life. She could hear his angry footsteps echoing down the deserted corridor outside. For a moment she was half tempted to jump out of bed and chase him, but she still couldn't think what to say.

She lay down again and stared up at the ceiling, virtually gnashing her teeth with fury. Little by little, however, the anger began to ebb, and one phrase he had uttered gradually came into the forefront of her brain, literally screaming for attention.

Had he actually said he'd fallen in love with her? She scarcely dared to believe it. It didn't matter. Even if he had indeed made the longed-for statement, it had definitely been in the past tense. It was too late now.

Two days later, Val stood by the window of her hospital room, fully dressed, gazing out at the hospital grounds, the lawn and shrubs gleaming in the thin January sunshine. Janet had stopped by the night before with clean clothes and a few toilet articles, and Val had been ready to leave since eight o'clock that morning.

She glanced impatiently at her watch. It was only eleven-thirty. Janet was due in an hour to pick her up, which gave her plenty of time to settle up the amount of her bill owing to the hospital over and above what her insurance would cover.

She hadn't seen Michael since that last dreadful scene, and by now her brain was numb from re-hashing it over and over again in her mind. She just wouldn't think about it, ever again. All she wanted was to get out of here, back to her home, her job, her life.

She went out into the corridor and started walking down to the business office at the far end. It felt good to be dressed again and out of that bed, but she was still slightly wobbly from the enforced inactivity, and stayed close to the wall, her eyes firmly fixed on her feet, in case she had a dizzy spell.

Suddenly, she came up against an immovable object directly in her path. She raised her eyes to see Michael standing before her, blocking her way. His expression was impenetrable, but he obviously had something on his mind and wasn't going to let her pass until he got it off his chest. She stood and waited.

'Do you have a way home?' he asked stiffly.

A sudden wave of tenderness for him flooded through her. In some mysterious fashion, known only to himself, this proud, stiff-necked man was offering her an olive-branch, by his lights probably even humbling himself. She thought quickly. What was she going to do about it?

'No,' she lied. 'I don't. I was going to call a cab.'

'I'll drive you, then,' he said in a flat tone of voice that brooked no disagreement.

'All right,' she said meekly. 'I still have to settle up at the office, but that should only take a few minutes.' She would also ask them to phone and explain to Janet.

Was she mistaken, or was that a look of relief, even gratitude, in the brilliant blue eyes? No matter. This was what she wanted. Taken completely off guard by the offer, she had no idea what he had in mind, but she did know with utter certainty that if there was a chance to be with him, for a day, a week, a year, a lifetime, this time she wasn't going to let it pass her by.

'Will you be ready to leave then?' he asked.

'Yes, my bag is all packed.'

'I'll go get it from your room, then, and will meet you at the office in a few minutes.'

He stepped out of her path and went past her, back the way she had come, towards her room, while she went on, her steps even more unsteady than before.

He didn't have much to say on the way home, except to ask directions and make mildly blasphemous comments on the Seattle traffic system and the incompetent drivers who clogged it.

At her building, he parked the car at the kerb out in front and came around to open the door for her. He reached down to pick up her bag with one hand, and grasped her firmly by the arm with the other to help her out of the car and up the path.

Her apartment was cold, the air dank and musty. Inside, Michael set her bag down just inside the entrance, then stood by the door watching her as she took off her coat and turned up the heat at the thermostat in the hall.

Val's mind was racing. She had no idea what had prompted him to offer to drive her home, but now that he was actually here, in her own living-room, her one thought was to keep him here. But how? Was the lift home only a polite gesture? She had to find out, and that meant taking a risk, making herself vulnerable to him. She would simply have to ask him.

She steeled herself and turned around to face him. He was standing just inside the door, a grave, attentive expression on his face, apparently waiting for her to say or do something to break the tension.

He looked so wonderful, so tall and strong. His coal-black hair was ruffled slightly from the strong breeze blowing outside, and she longed to go to him, to throw her arms around him and beg him not to leave.

But she was paralysed with indecision and fear. She couldn't move, couldn't speak. Finally, he turned towards the door and put his hand on the knob. Her heart sank. He was going to leave. When he opened his mouth to speak, she knew it was going to be to say goodbye.

'Well, Val, do you need any shopping done?' he asked politely. 'Groceries, anything like that?'

'No, thanks,' she mumbled in some confusion. 'I keep a pretty good stock of frozen and canned foods on hand.'

He smiled, for the first time that day. 'Well, then, perhaps we could rustle up something for lunch. I don't know about you, but I'm starved.'

It was the last thing she had expected. Somehow, his offhand tone and slightly proprietorial air, his calm assumption that he had the right to be there, disarmed her completely, and the last vestige of reserve and mistrust fled from her mind. In its place there rose within her a wild, intense surge of hope. In the next moment, she burst into tears.

Instantly, he had crossed the ten feet or so that separated them and was by her side. His arms came around her, and she pressed her wet face into his chest, gulping and sniffing.

'Hey,' he murmured into her ear. 'What's this? Come on, Val, there's nothing to cry about. I know I've behaved badly to you, and I'm sorry. I'll try to make it up to you if you'll let me. But please, I can't stand to hear you cry.'

When she finally regained control, she raised her tear-stained face to his. 'Michael, what are you saying?'

His jaw hardened, and a little pulse began to beat just below his ear. 'I'm saying that I want you to let me back into your life. I'm saying I care for you. Damn it, Val, I love you.'

She could hardly believe her ears. 'But I thought——'

'I know what you thought,' he broke in with an impatient wave of his hand. 'I already agreed that I've behaved badly to you, but can't you admit that your paranoia might have played some part in our difficulties?'

'Oh, of course I do!' she cried angrily. 'I could kick myself when I think of all the time we've wasted, largely because of my own childish fears. I still don't really understand it. It just seemed that since my father and David had let me down, the two most important men in my life, I didn't dare trust anyone. Then, when I found out from Myra that you were only using me——'

'But it wasn't like that,' he broke in heatedly. 'I admit I started out with that stupid idea in my mind. My grief over David's death was largely guilt. I was angry and needed a target, and there you were. But I came to my senses when I saw what a genuine, caring person you were underneath all that frosty reserve.' He smiled down at her warmly. 'An independent little soul, too, taking care of yourself all alone in the world without whining. I liked that.'

She sighed. 'All my life I thought the one important thing was to be safe, to protect myself. I don't think it was until the accident when I was lying there in the hospital, helpless, that I realised there was only one person in the whole city, Janet, whom I could call on to take me home. Oh, I knew a lot of people, of course, but I was close to no one.'

He gathered her closer in his arms. 'Well, I'm going to change all that,' he murmured. 'But you must trust me. Can't we put all that behind us at last? Please, Val. I need you so badly, and I love you so much.'

She gazed up into his eyes. 'Michael, do you mean it? This isn't a dream, is it? When you stalked out of my room the other night I was positive I'd never see you again.'

He smiled down at her. 'You mean something like the "ravings" of a concussed patient?'

She reddened deeply. 'Well——'

He put a finger on her lips. 'Never mind. I knew damned good and well you were lying when you claimed it was all a drug-induced hallucination. I probably should have stayed and forced you to admit it, but you've played such merry hell with my ego in the last five months that I just saw red.' He shrugged.

'Besides, I'm a doctor. You'd been through a severe trauma and were still weak.'

'Well, you were right,' she admitted. 'I did mean every word. But, Michael, I was so sure you didn't care that I couldn't admit the truth.' She raised her chin and gave him a challenging look. 'After all, you seemed to be pretty deeply involved with Diana Worth.'

'Diana!' he exclaimed. He looked down at her incredulously. 'Diana means nothing to me. We were thrown together because of her grandfather's position on the hospital board.' He grinned. 'Actually, she was primarily a means to get to you.'

'How was I to know that? I didn't even realise you were in town until I read about it in the newspaper.'

'I intended to approach you gradually. You were so angry when you left me last summer that I was afraid I'd scare you off if I rushed you. Then later, when we met at that blasted party for Diana's grandfather, and you claimed you wanted to be friends, or at least not enemies, I felt it was hopeless.'

She remembered that party vividly. 'What else could I do? You were so cold and distant that night. I thought you hated me for the things I said last summer about your failings as a brother. Then that night in the restaurant, just before Christmas, your own parting words were that you hoped we could be friends.'

'At the time I figured that was better than nothing. At least it was a possible way back into your life.' He drew back from her and gave her a stern, accusing look. 'And if I seemed cold at that blasted party, perhaps you've forgotten that you showed up with that idiot Don Carter hanging all over you.' He paused for a moment, his jaw set and grim, then said, 'Perhaps you'd care to tell me about that.'

Her eyes widened in disbelief, then she broke out laughing. 'Don Carter! You must be joking!'

His dark eyebrows shot up. 'Well, let's not think about Don Carter now. I want you to focus all your attention on me.'

She cocked her head to one side and smiled up at him. 'And just what did you have in mind?'

'Come here,' he murmured, 'and I'll show you.'

There was no mistaking the shining light of desire in the blazing blue eyes as he bent his head. His mouth opened over hers, pulling gently at her lips, over and over again, in a rhythmic motion that lulled her mind and inflamed her senses at the same time. She melted against him, the hard body taut against hers.

Suddenly, with a low groan deep in his throat, his mouth opened wider and his tongue pushed past her lips, hungry, demanding, seeking. Val was filled with a blissful drowning sensation, where the only realities were his hard body grinding against hers, the heat of his mouth, the strong arms enfolding her.

After several long, wonderful moments, he drew his head back and gazed down into her eyes, his breath coming in short bursts, his heart pounding wildly against hers. He spread the fingers of one hand around the base of her neck, the palm flat against her upper chest. Gradually, in a slow, seductive movement, his eyes never leaving hers, he lowered his hand until it came to rest on one firm, full breast.

'I want you so badly, darling,' he ground out. 'One more second of this and it'll be too late. If you want to stop, it had better be right now.'

She smiled up at him. 'Now,' was all she said.

She moved out of his arms. Taking him by the hand, she led the way down the hall to her bedroom. The blinds were drawn, casting the room in pale shadows. At the side of the bed she turned to him and slipped her arms around his waist.

'Are you sure, Val?' he asked huskily. 'It'll be hell, but if you'd rather wait until we can get married, I'll understand.'

She shook her head and put her fingers on his lips. 'I'm sure,' she breathed. 'I love you, Michael. And I do want you. All of you.'

To prove it, she reached up, loosened his tie, and started slowly unbuttoning his shirt to reveal the broad, smooth chest, tanned and firmly muscled. As she ran her hands over it, she could feel his skin quivering under her touch.

He reached out for her, clutching at her eagerly, tearing at her clothes, and as his mouth covered hers they sank down slowly together on to the bed.

Some time later, Val awoke to the sound of rain slashing against the bedroom window. In that first instant of consciousness, she automatically listened for the familiar hospital sounds, but as her eyes fluttered open she realised that she was home again, in her own room, her own bed.

Then she gradually became aware of the man lying beside her, the strong, hard body almost touching hers, and the memory of their hour of passion came flooding back. She glanced over at him. He was lying on his back, deeply asleep, his black hair tousled, a peaceful expression on his face. His arms lay at his sides outside the covers, leaving his chest and shoulders bare, and she could only stare, marvelling at the sheer beauty of the man, her heart full of a love that was painful in its intensity.

As she nestled down beside him, he stirred slightly in his sleep, muttering under his breath, and one long arm came around her waist, his large hand warm and firm on her bare skin. She covered his hand with hers and closed her eyes.

It's by finding the courage to take risks and to make ourselves vulnerable to another human being, she mused dreamily, that we're most safe. Michael had hurt her unjustly by trying to get even with her for something she hadn't done. But in a peculiar way it was that very desire for revenge—a bittersweet revenge—that had brought them together.

She only knew she loved him with all her heart and that to love meant to trust. It was true that a girl could get hurt that way, she thought, as Michael's hand began to move lazily over her body, but look what she would miss without it.

Holiday Habits Questionnaire

A Free Mills & Boon Romance for you!

At Mills & Boon we always do our best to ensure that our books are just what you want to read. To do this we need your help! Please spare a few minutes to answer the questions below and overleaf and, as a special thank you, we will send you a FREE Mills & Boon Romance when you return your completed questionnaire.

We'd like to find out about your holiday habits and holiday reading, so that we can continue to provide you with the high quality Romances you have come to expect.

Don't forget to fill in your name and address so we know where to send your FREE BOOK.

Please tick the appropriate boxes to indicate your answers. ☑

1 How many hoildays do you have a year?

None ❑ 1 ❑ 2 ❑ 3 ❑ More than 3 ❑

2 Have you been on holiday within the last year? Yes ❑ No ❑

3 If YES where did you go?________________

4 When taking holidays do you normally go? (tick only one)

(a) Europe ❑ (b) U.K. ❑
(c) Outside Europe ❑ (d) Other ________________

Please complete overleaf

5 **How do you usually travel to your holiday destination?** (tick only one)

(a) Coach ❑ (b) Train ❑ (c) Plane ❑
(d) Boat ❑ (e) Car ❑

6 **What type of holiday do you usually have while you are away?**

(a) Coach ❑ (b) Caravan ❑ (c) Hotel ❑
(d) Holiday Camp ❑ (e) Bed and Breakfast ❑ (f) Villa ❑
(g) Other ______

7 **Do you usually take a Mills & Boon Romance with you?** Yes ❑ No ❑

(a) If YES, How many? 1 ❑ 2-4 ❑ 4+ ❑
(b) If NO - Do you take any other books? Yes ❑ No ❑

Type of book e.g. mystery, biography.

______

8 **Do you buy books while you are away?** Yes ❑ No ❑

9 **Which age group are you in?**

Under 25 ❑ 25-34 ❑
35-54 ❑ 55-65 ❑

Over 65 please state ______

10 **Are you a Reader Service subscriber?**

Yes ❑ No ❑
If YES Sub No. ______

Thank you for your help. We hope that you enjoy your FREE book.

Post this page TODAY TO: Mills & Boon Reader Survey FREEPOST, P.O. Box 236, Croydon CR9 9EL. (No stamp required)

EDQ4

Mrs/Ms/Miss/Mr ______

Address ______

______

______

______ Postcode ______

You may be mailed with offers from Mills & Boon Ltd. and other respected companies as a result of replying. If you would prefer not to share this opportunity please write and tell us.